Abigale
The Carmichaels
Leigh Fenty

Chapter One

"Hmm. Seems to be a pattern."

Abby had five weeks left. Five weeks until she could return to the Starlight Ranch and never leave again. That is if Deacon kept his word. They had a deal. She promised to give college one more year. He promised he'd let her drop out of if she was still unhappy. She'd done her year. Or all but five weeks of it. She was ready to go home.

Abby was sitting in the dining hall with her friend, Adam, who'd she met last semester. She considered him a friend, but she knew he wanted more from her. He was sweet, polite, and respectful. All the things she should want in a man. But she wasn't interested. He was from Houston. A city boy who had no idea what her life was like in Connelly. He'd never pushed her, or asked her for more than she was willing to give. It seemed she was destined to be friends with nice men. She was beginning to see a pattern.

She smiled at him. "So, I'm not looking forward to that English assignment."

"Poetry. Not a problem. It's so subjective you can write anything you want and no one can judge you."

"I'm pretty sure Professor Evans will judge the hell out of me."

Adam laughed. "Just write something about horses. Or your beloved ranch you miss so much."

"No." She took a sip of her soda. "That'll just make me sad."

"A few more weeks of school left. You're almost there."

"And I can't wait."

He took her hand. "I really wish you'd let me take you out at least once before you're gone for the summer."

"We're out right now."

He looked around the school cantina. "Eating in the cafeteria isn't a date."

She gave Adam a smile. She figured she owed him one date. "Maybe we could go get pizza or something."

"Only if it's just you and me and not a group of people."

"Fine. Just you and me. A goodbye pizza."

He put a hand over his heart. "Abby, you're killing me."

She'd told him this was her last semester and that she wouldn't be coming back. But it seemed he didn't quite believe her. She cocked her head. "I miss my horses."

"I just hope you miss me as much as you miss your damn horses."

"I'll keep in touch." It seemed like the right thing to say to him. But she knew she probably wouldn't. Once she was home, Georgetown, the university, and everybody she'd met over the last three semesters would be a faded memory.

When a girl they both knew came up to the table, Abby gave her a smile. "Hi, Beth."

"Hi." She glanced at Adam, then looked back at Abby. "There's a really cute guy in a cowboy hat looking for you."

"Really? Hmm." She smiled at Adam. "I guess I should go see who it is."

She got to her feet, and so did Adam. "I'll come with."

When she went outside and saw who it was standing next to a pickup, she gasped.

Adam frowned. "Who is it?"

"My brother."

"I thought your family lived up north."

"They do." Tanner spotted Abby and gave her a wave. She let go of Adam's hand and ran across the grass to Tanner and hugged him. "What are you doing here?" She stepped back and looked at him. "What's wrong? Is it Cassidy or the baby?"

Tanner shook his head. "Can we go somewhere more private to talk?"

Abby put her hands on her hips. "Tanner Joseph, tell me why you're here."

He sighed and looked around, before taking her arm and moving her to the truck door. "Get in and I'll tell you."

She got in the driver's side door, then slid across the seat. "What's wrong?"

He got in and took her hand. She'd always been able to read her little brother's face. And today it was telling her something was very wrong.

"It's mother."

"Is she ill?"

He shook his head and said, barely above a whisper, "Mother's gone."

Abby stared at him for a moment, not quite contemplating what he'd said. "Gone?" Finally, she realized what he was saying. "She's...gone? She's...?" She covered her face with her hands, and Tanner pulled her in for a hug. He held her for a few minutes while the first initial wave of grief consumed her.

When she'd gained some control, he said, "Deacon didn't want to tell you on the phone. And he couldn't leave Cassidy, not with the baby coming so soon."

Abby moved back away from him and swiped at the tears on her face. "I'm glad it was you. Thank you for driving all the way here to tell me."

He nodded, then opened the glove box and handed her a napkin. She wiped her eyes, then laid her head on his shoulder for several minutes while the news of her mother's passing sunk in.

Faith had been merely surviving for the last eleven and a half years. The last two she'd spent more and more time inside of her head. It was a world where her husband was still alive. Since Deacon and

Cassidy got married not quite a year ago, Faith had been permanently altered. She'd missed the wedding and everything since. She had no idea she was about to become a grandmother. But she'd always been otherwise healthy, so her passing was unexpected.

Abby looked at Tanner. "How?"

He shrugged. "She just didn't wake up."

"When?"

"Yesterday morning."

Abby gasped again. Her mother had been dead for a whole day and she didn't know it. She hadn't felt it. How is that possible? How could she not have sensed some shift in the universe?

"I'm coming home with you."

"I figured."

It was suddenly clear what she had to do. "For good. I'm not coming back."

Tanner pushed her back and looked at her. "This is hardly the time to make that decision."

"I not coming back." She was done being told what to do. "There are only five weeks left. I'll finish online. Or I won't finish. I don't care. I'm going home.

He nodded. "Okay. What do we need to do to get you out of here?"

She kissed him on the cheek. "Thank you for not..."

"Being Deacon?"

She gave him a small smile. "I need to clear out my dorm, and go to the admission's office."

"Okay. Where's the dorm?"

When she saw Adam standing several feet away, she patted Tanner's arm. "I'll be right back. I need to say bye to my friend." She got out of the truck and went to Adam.

He looked at her closely. "Are you okay?"

"My brother's here to take me home."

"Home? What are you talking about?"

Abby hugged him while she tried not to cry again. "My mother died yesterday."

He tighten his grip on her and rubbed her back. "I'm so sorry. What can I do?"

She stepped away from him and dabbed at her eyes. "Nothing. But I didn't want to leave without saying goodbye."

"But you'll be back, right?"

She shook her head. "No. I won't be back."

"Abby."

"I know. I'm sorry. My family needs me."

Adam nodded and like the good guy he was, he said, "Of course."

"I've got to go."

"Call me. Let me know you got there."

She nodded. "Bye, Adam." She got back in the truck and Tanner looked through the windshield at Adam.

"Boyfriend?"

"No. Just friends."

"Hmm. Seems to be a pattern."

She nudged him. "Just drive."

They drove to the dorms, and Tanner followed Abby upstairs to her room. Deacon had told her she could get an apartment, but she wanted to stay in the dorms. It kept her on campus and she didn't need her car. An apartment would've been too much of a commitment. She'd never felt committed to being in college. She'd hated it since day one.

The room was a mess, which seemed to surprise Tanner. Her room at home was always neat and tidy. But this wasn't her room at home. This was her dorm room, and she didn't care how it looked.

He looked a little overwhelmed. "Looks like a Texas tornado went through here."

"Yeah. It sort of does."

He took off his hat and dropped it on the bed, then ran a hand through his blonde hair. "Where do we start?"

"I've got all of my boxes. I broke them down just waiting for the day I could fill them up again. We need to tape them and fill them."

She pulled a stack of flattened boxes from under her bed. "Here you go." She took a roll of tape from the desk drawer. "You tape. I'll start throwing out stuff I don't want." She also had trash bags in the desk and she started filling one up. She wasn't being too selective. She didn't care about any of this stuff. It represented a life she didn't want.

In an hour, they had four bags of trash and all the boxes were full. There was a stash of stuff in one corner, which she'd leave for anyone who might want it. It was standard procedure when someone moved out before the end of the semester.

When she saw someone she knew pass by, she went to the door. "Sandy?" The woman turned around. "I'm moving out. There's some stuff in here, if you want first dibs.

Sandy came to her. "Moving out? Where are you going?"

"Home. I can't get into it. But I'm going home." She saw Sandy checking out Tanner. "This is my brother, Tanner."

Sandy smiled. "Hi."

Tanner nodded and Abby patted Sandy's arm. "He's my *little* brother. Just about to graduate from high school."

Sandy frowned. "Do you have any older brothers?"

"Two, and they're both taken."

Sandy sighed, then hugged Abby. "I'm going to miss you. Don't tell anyone else about your stuff. I want to go through it first."

Abby gave her a hug, then turned to Tanner. "Okay. Now we need to haul them downstairs."

He picked up a box. "Let's go."

Abby picked up another box and followed him. Having three big strong brothers often came in handy. It took them another thirty minutes to load her boxes in the back of the truck. And when they were done, Tanner looked at her.

"Is there anyone else you want to say goodbye to?"

"No. Let's go."

"What about the admission's office?

"I'll call them. I just want to go home."

It was almost an eight-hour drive home and Tanner asked Abby if she wanted to spend the night somewhere, but she wanted to go straight home.

She looked at him. "I'm sorry. When did you leave? Did you sleep last night?"

"I pulled over and slept for a few hours. I'm good."

"We'll if you get tired, I can drive."

Tanner nodded. "Maybe later." Like Tobias and Deacon, he didn't like being the passenger in his own truck. It was a long and boring drive, but they spent the time reminiscing about better days with their mother. Despite her withdrawal, there were some good times to remember.

They pulled into Connelly at eight and got to the ranch twenty minutes later. Tanner had texted Deacon when they got to Connelly, so when they pulled into the driveway, everyone was waiting on the porch as they drove up to the house. Deacon came to open the door, and Abby got out and hugged him. Seeing him brought back the tears.

"I can't believe she's gone."

He held her for a few moments, then kissed her on the forehead. "I'm glad you're here."

She nodded, then went to Tobias and hugged him.

"Hey, sis. Welcome home."

She looked up at him. "Did you get taller while I was away?"

"No. I think you got shorter. All that city air."

She kissed him on the cheek, then went to Cassidy. She kissed her and her nine and a half month baby bump. Next, she went to Gemma. Last but not least, she hugged Riley, who had actually gotten a bit taller.

She stood back and wiped her eyes. "I missed you all so much."

Deacon put his arm around her. "Let's get you inside." He glanced at Tanner. "Did you guys eat?"

"We had a burger about four hours ago."

"That's what I figured. Ruthie made chili today."

They went to the dining room, and Ruthie came in and hugged Abby, too, then sniffled and wiped her eyes. "You two sit now. I'll get your dinner."

Tanner and Abby sat along with Cassidy and Gemma. Tobias took Riley's hand.

"I need to get this young man to bed."

"I don't want to go home yet. They just got here."

"We're not going home. We're staying in the guest rooms. Come on now. Abby will be here a while. You can see her in the morning."

Abby smiled at Riley. "Come here my sweet little nephew."

Riley kissed Abby goodnight, then left with Tobias.

She smiled at Gemma. "Seems my brother has taken to step-fatherhood quite well."

"He's great. They're best buddies. So much so, that I feel left out sometimes."

Abby laughed. "As someone who has spent her whole life on the outside of the Carmichael Boys Club. I know exactly what you mean."

Ruthie brought in two bowls of chili and a plate of cornbread. She set them down in front of Tanner and Abby, then looked at the rest of them. "Seems to me, the women are gaining in numbers. The three of you ladies. And that little one in Miss Cassidy's tummy. You girls can start giving these boys a run for their money."

Gemma smiled. "You're right, Ruthie. And you're the honorary president of the club."

"I'd be honored. Now. Is anyone else hungry again?"

Deacon shook his head. "I'm okay. But I imagine Tobias might want a bowl."

Gemma nodded. "I'm sure he will."

"You're sure I will what?" Tobias came in and squeezed her shoulders.

"Want some chili."

He nodded. "Yes, ma'am."

Ruthie left, and Tobias sat next to Gemma.

As everyone ate, it was quiet and Abby wanted to break the uncomfortable silence.

"So, what's the plan? What are we doing for her?"

Deacon, who was still standing next to Cassidy, went to the end of the table and sat down.

"She didn't want a funeral. No fuss, she said. We'll take her ashes and put them with Dad's."

Abby nodded. "Good. I like that. When?"

"Day after tomorrow."

"Okay."

Tobias pushed his bowl aside. "Tomorrow, I'll take you up to the house if you'd like. Gemma has been busy. It's looking really good."

"I can't wait to see it. It looked pretty good at Christmas, though."

"We've got a garden space cleared out and tilled. And a greenhouse full of tiny little plants. Ready to plant as soon as we're past the frost danger."

"You had a cold winter this year."

"We did. More snow than we've had in years."

Gemma smiled. "Which Riley loved."

Abby looked at Cassidy. "And that baby is due really soon, right?"

"I'm a week away from my due date."

"Oh my goodness. I can't wait." She looked at Deacon. "Are you ready, Dad?"

He smiled. "I'm definitely ready to meet our little girl."

"And do you have a name yet?"

"We do." He looked at Cassidy. "But we're keeping it under wraps. We want her to be the first one to hear it."

Abby tried not to let that make her emotional again. "That's really sweet. I love it."

Tobias leaned back in his chair. "Tanner and I have a wager going. We each have a list of possible names. If the name is on one of our lists, we win."

"And what do you win?"

"Dinner at the restaurant of our choice."

"And what if you both lose?"

"Then we'll probably still go to dinner. Maybe we'll even bring you."

"Gee, I feel so honored."

"I guarantee you, her name won't be on either of your lists." Deacon got to his feet and looked at Cassidy. "You should probably go get some sleep, hon." He went to her and helped her to her feet. "I'll be up in a few minutes."

Cassidy smiled at Abby. "I'll see you all in the morning."

Tanner stood, too. "I'm bushed. I'm going to bed, too."

Abby took his hand. "Thank you for coming to get me."

"Of course."

Gemma looked at Tobias. "We should call it a night, too."

He nodded and glanced at Deacon. "Yeah. See you guys tomorrow."

Abby watched them go, then looked at Deacon. "Somehow, I think that was prearranged."

Deacon sat across from her and smiled. "I figured you might have something you want to talk to me about."

She leaned back in her chair. "Well, I was going to wait for a better time to do it."

"No time like the present. Let me hear it."

She took a breath. "I don't want to go back. I moved out of my dorm. I have everything with me. I don't care what you say. I'm not going back." She swiped at a tear, not sure why she was, once more, getting emotional.

"Abby."

"What? You said to give it a year. And I did. Or at least I almost did."

"Abby. It's fine."

"What do you mean it's fine? What's fine? That I'm asking? Or that I can stay home."

"Both."

She got up and ran around the table, then threw her arms around his neck. "Thank you."

"Sit down."

She sat in the chair next to him. "You did what I asked. You gave it more time. Mother's passing has given me a different perspective. Time is precious. Family is precious. You, my little sister, are precious. I want you to be happy. And, honestly, I've missed the hell out of you."

She reached for his hand. "I don't want to miss any part of the baby coming."

"You want to see me change diapers and rock my little girl to sleep?"

"Yes."

"Well, I'm not too sure about the diaper changing. But I'm totally down for the rocking to sleep part."

She squeezed his hand. "You're going to be a great dad."

"How do you know that?"

"Because you've raised me since I was ten."

"It was my pleasure. I hope I wasn't too hard on you."

She smiled. "You were. But it's okay."

"You've turned into a hell of a woman, Abby."

She cocked her head. "I thought I was always going to be sixteen to you."

"You are." He nodded. "You are."

Chapter Two

"Nah. I don't want to tarnish his halo."

Deacon came into the room and found Cassidy in bed. She was lying on her side, which was the only way she could be semi-comfortable. After slipping off his boots, he laid down next to her. He kissed her neck, then began rubbing her lower back.

She smiled. "Mmm. Thank you. How'd that go?"

"Abby is officially done with college."

She glanced over her shoulder at him. "And how do you feel about that?"

"It's fine. She's been miserable for a year and a half."

"She must be very happy."

He moved some hair from Cassidy's cheek and kissed her. "So does everyone think I've been an ogre about the whole college thing?"

She laughed. "Pretty much, yeah."

"Shit. I was just trying to honor our father's dream for his children."

Cassidy rolled onto her back. "I know. We all know. You are the backbone of this family, and we all love you for it."

He rubbed her belly. "I want to be a good dad. I don't want to fail this little girl."

She took his hand and moved it to where he could feel the baby moving. "That is not even a possibility."

He sighed. "I guess we'll find out."

"If she ever decides to leave the nest and make an appearance."

He smiled at her. "You're not even due yet."

"Oh, I'm due. I'm so due."

Deacon laughed. "So, are you re-thinking the big family idea?"

She thought about it for a moment. "No. As soon as this one comes out and gets past the needy infant stage. I'll be ready again."

"Hmm."

Cassidy looked at him. "Is that a hmm, I agree? Or a hmm, I'm not so sure?"

"It's a hmm, I love you and you should get some sleep."

"And you better get up and get undressed before you fall asleep in your clothes."

It won't be the first time." He got off the bed and headed for the bathroom. "I'll be right back."

"Deacon?"

He stopped and looked at her.

"You did the right thing with Abby."

"I hope so."

"She got to experience college. She got to see a different life than what she's got here. It's only made her appreciate home more."

He pointed at her. "Right. That's exactly why I made her go."

Cassidy laughed. "No, it's not. You did it because you're an ogre."

"An ogre, huh?"

"A really handsome ogre. Get undressed and come back to bed."

Deacon grinned. "If you weren't nine plus months pregnant, I'd consider that an invitation."

"I'll give you a rain check."

"Seems I have a stack of those now."

"Don't worry, Cowboy. I'm good for it."

Abby was tired from the drive and the emotional day. But she couldn't sleep. Now that she was home, the reality of her mother's passing seemed more real. Even though Faith hadn't played much of a part in their lives since their father died, it was still comforting to know she was there in the house. At any time, if Abby wanted to see her, all she had to do was go to her room. Now she wished she'd done it more often.

Abby sat up and threw back her covers and got out of bed. She stepped into her slippers and put on a robe, then headed downstairs. She paused for a moment at her mother's door, then slowly opened it. The window shades were open, and the moon gave enough light so that she could make out the furniture. For as long as she could remember, the room had been the same. And even without the moonlight she could've made her way to the couch without running into anything.

When she heard, "Hey, sis," she squinted at the couch.

"Tobias?"

"Yeah. The one and only."

She moved to the couch and could see him sitting there with his feet on the coffee table.

"What are you doing in here?"

He looked up at her. "I imagine the same thing you are."

She dropped down next to him, leaned back, and put her slippered feet next to his boots. "I can't believe she's gone."

"Mother's been gone for a long time, Abby."

She took his hand. Of the four of them, Tobias had always had the most difficulty dealing with their mother's lack of involvement in their lives.

"But she was here. In this room. It was comforting to know that."

"Hmm." He sighed. "She must've really loved him."

"Yeah."

"To ignore your kids for eleven years. To miss your son's wedding. To miss your grandchild being born." He dropped his feet to the ground and leaned forward to put his face in his hands. "It pisses me off, Abby. I know that makes me a bastard. But it pisses me off."

She put a hand on his back. "Who are you really mad at, Tobias? Mom? Or Yourself?"

He sat up and looked at her. "What do you mean?"

"I think maybe you're feeling a little guilty for being mad at her for eleven years."

"I'm haven't been..." He leaned back again. "I could've been a better son."

"She knew you loved her."

He put his feet back up on the table. "I was a little shit for a lot of years. I caused her more pain. Added to her misery."

"Well, I think Deacon was the one who had to deal with you being a little shit. Mother wasn't always aware of what you were up to. Deacon kept it from her."

"Deacon. You're lucky he was your oldest brother. If you only had me, God knows where we'd be right now."

She took his hand. "We'd be fine. Because you would've done what you had to do. Just like Deacon did. I'm sure he would've much rather preferred to hang out with you and get into trouble. At least for a while."

Tobias laughed. "He did let himself go once in a while."

"Really. Do tell."

"Nah. I don't want to tarnish his halo."

She studied his profile in the moonlight. "You have a halo, too, you know. It's just slips to the side every once in a while."

He turned and looked at her. "How's it looking right now?"

"Pretty straight. Gemma and Riley have been good for you."

"God, I love them. That kid. What a trip he is."

"So, when are you two going to get married?"

"Hey. I offered. She just hasn't accepted."

"She will."

"It doesn't really matter one way or the other. We can live in sin for the rest of our lives. I'm fine with that."

"I don't believe they call it that anymore. It's quite acceptable to live with someone without getting married."

He looked at her. "So, how about you? Did you break some hearts in Georgetown?"

"No. I wasn't too interested in those city boys."

"There had to be a better selection than there is here. Deacon and I got lucky with women from out of the area. Not sure you can depend on that to happen again."

"I'm in no hurry."

"Good to know. There's no rush. Take your time. Find the right guy."

She smiled at him. "And by the right guy, you mean someone you, Deacon, and Tanner approve of."

"Damn right."

Abby laughed. "I'm going to be single for a really long time."

She and Tobias stayed and talked for a while longer, then they both left their mother's room and went to bed. When she settled into bed, she finally felt tired. She was home. For good. Deacon finally listened to her.

She didn't blame him, and she had to admit to herself it was a good experience to have. She met a few interesting people. Learned some stuff she didn't know. And got to experience life away from the ranch. But she was glad to be back. This is where she belonged.

She slept in and when she went downstairs in the morning, everyone was in the dining room eating breakfast.

Tanner looked at her. "Glad you could join us."

"I'm sorry. You should've gotten me up."

Cassidy smiled at her. "You were tired. You needed the rest."

Tanner frowned. "I drove there and back, and I managed to get up this morning in time for breakfast."

Ruthie came in and set a plate down in front of her. "Give the poor girl a break. She just needs a few days to adjust to ranch life again."

Abby smiled. "Yeah. That. That's it. I'm adjusting. Thank you, Ruthie."

Tobias took a drink of coffee. "So, do you want to take a ride with me to the house, today?"

"Yeah. When?"

"This afternoon. Tanner and I are working with a horse this morning."

Abby looked at Tanner. "What about school?"

"I'm taking the week off."

"Oh. Right. Of course." She took a bite of scrambled eggs. "Maybe I'll go into town this morning. Does anybody need anything?"

Deacon looked around the table. "I think we're all good. Cassidy and I need to go in later for a doctor's appointment."

"Okay. I won't be gone long."

Tanner grinned. "Are you planning on taking the long way in past the Fremont ranch by any chance?"

"Shut up. I haven't talked to Skyler in a couple of months now."

Tanner glanced at Deacon. "Hmm. Well, he's around, I guess. We haven't seen much of him either."

She missed Skyler and she was sorry they'd lost touch. He wasn't home for the Christmas holidays. And after that, the calls and texts started dropping off. "I might call him in a few days. Just to let him know I'm back."

Tobias nodded. "Sounds like a solid plan, Abby."

"Okay, fine. I'll admit that I miss him. He wasn't here when I came home for Christmas. I haven't seen him since last fall."

Deacon gave her a small smile. "You should definitely let him know you're back."

Abby wanted to change the subject. "What horse are you working with?"

Tobias leaned back in his chair. "Pale Rider."

"Who is that?"

"The horse Deacon bought out from under Winston at the auction a year-and-a-half ago. That's his new name." He glance at Cassidy. "It's been changed a few times."

Cassidy smiled. "I couldn't decide on the perfect name."

Deacon put his arm on the back of Cassidy's chair. "He's going to make a damn good jumper."

Cassidy glanced at him. "Which means he's actually Deacon's horse."

"What's mine is yours, my love."

Abby set her fork down. "I'd like to see him in action." She looked at Tobias. "You're not jumping him, are you?"

"As much as it kills me, not to, no." He glanced at Gemma. "But someday, soon. I'm going to give it a try."

Gemma patted his leg. "We've made some pretty good progress with Tobias' leg."

"Well, it helps to live with a talented physical therapist."

Abby looked at Riley. "I bet you're quite the horseman now."

He smiled. "Yeah. I'm really good. I have my own horse."

"I know. Tobias told me. You'll have to introduce me to him."

"I'm a cowboy just like Tobias."

Tobias winked at him. "Yes, you are."

After breakfast, Abby drove into town. Even though she was tempted, she didn't take the long way into town to drive by Skyler's family ranch. It was fifteen miles out of the way and it wouldn't have done her much good to drive by the entrance. The ranch house was two miles from the road. She'd only been to the Fremont ranch one time. She'd spent a fair amount of time with Skyler since he came back from Harvard, but it was always in town or at the Starlight. She didn't care much for his parents, and she didn't like how Skyler was around them. He was much too eager to bend to their wishes. Maybe it wasn't eagerness. Maybe it was fear. Either way, he was much more fun to be around, away from them.

She parked at the end of town and got out to walk. Connelly was small, with one main street through town. There was a streetlight in the middle of it where the other main thoroughfare crossed it. It had been a four-way stop pretty much since cars were first introduced in town. But five years ago, the town council voted to put a traffic light in the middle of town. Last Abby heard, there had been more accidents at the intersection since the light was put in, than before.

She headed down the sidewalk, taking her time, greeting people she knew, and looking in shop windows. As a teenager, she hated how small Connelly was. Now she loved it. When she saw a familiar face headed her way, she stopped walking, as did he.

"Skyler?"

He released the hand of the woman walking next to him and went to Abby.

"Abby. I'm so sorry about your mother." He hugged her and held it for a moment, then let go and stepped back.

Abby wiped away a stray tear. Since she'd gotten the news of her mother's passing, it didn't take much to start them flowing. "It's so good to see you." She glanced at the woman. She wasn't from Connelly, and Abby instantly didn't like her.

Skyler glanced over his shoulder. "Oh." He reached for the woman's hand. "This is Rebecca Greenwood."

Rebecca gave Abby a cool smile and offered her hand. "I'm Skyler's fiancé."

Chapter Three

"It never occurred to me to interfere."

When Abby pulled up to the barn, all three of her brothers were at the large training pen. Tanner was on Pale Rider, and Deacon and Tobias were sitting on the fence. Abby got out of her car and strode over to them. She stopped a few feet away with her hands on her hips.

"So, I guess you all thought it was pretty damn funny."

Deacon turned around and looked at her as Tobias jumped to the ground. "What are you talking about, Abby?"

She took on Deacon's tone. "Oh, you should definitely let him know you're in town, Abby." She scowled. "I hope you all had a good laugh after I left."

Tobias took a few steps toward her. "Sis, we have no idea what or who you're talking about."

"Skyler. Skyler and his fiancé. *Rebecca* Greenwood."

"Whoa. What? We had no idea." He glanced at Deacon. "Or at least I had no idea."

Deacon jumped to the ground and Abby glared at him. "You knew? And you didn't tell me?"

"Abby."

She raised her hand. "There's no excuse."

"I figured you knew. I figured he told you. I didn't know you hadn't talked in a while."

"Well, we haven't. And he didn't." She looked at Tanner. "Did you know?"

Tanner shook his head. "No one ever tells me anything."

Tobias went to her and put a hand on her shoulder. "How'd you find out?"

She stepped away from him. "I ran into him and *her* in town."

Tanner walked Pale Rider to the fence. "Weren't you trying to find Skyler a wife last spring at Deacon's wedding?"

Deacon glanced at Tanner and shook his head. "Not now, Tanner."

Abby folded her arms across her chest. "She's all wrong for him. There's no way he actually loves her."

Tobias cocked his head. "Didn't you just meet her?"

"Yes. But when I got back to the car, I googled her and her pretentious family. They're just like the Fremonts. He'd basically be marrying a woman who is like his mother." She growled. "He hates his mother."

Tobias smiled, but stopped when she frowned at him. "Abby. He's a grown man. I'm sure he hasn't let his parents talk him into marrying someone he doesn't want to marry."

"You know how his parents are. He's not a grown man when he's around them."

Deacon walked up beside Tobias. "Maybe he's marrying her because she's available and willing."

Abby raised an eyebrow. "What's that supposed to mean?"

"The man has only had eyes for you since he came back from Harvard. You shunned him. You locked him into the friend zone. At some point, he had to move on."

"Not this again. How he does or doesn't feel about me is beside the point. He can't marry her."

Tobias smiled. "So, what are you going to do about it?"

She took a deep breath. "I don't know yet."

Tanner nodded toward the driveway. "You might think about it. Here he comes."

Abby turned to see Skyler's car driving past the house. He parked next to her car and got out. He looked at the four Carmichael siblings, hesitated for a moment, then started walking toward them.

Abby looked at her brothers. "Just let me handle it."

Tobias nodded and Deacon raised a hand. "It never occurred to me to interfere."

Abby turned and walked toward Skyler. When she got to him, she took his arm and steered him away from the training pen. They headed down the path toward the pond. They were both quiet until they got to the water.

Abby let go of his arm, stopped walking, and turned to him. "When were you going to tell me? Was I just going to get a wedding invitation in the mail one day?"

"Abby. I wanted to tell you. But I didn't want to do it in a text or email. Even over the phone seemed wrong."

"How long have you been engaged? When I left in August, you were a single man."

"We've been engaged since February."

"Three months. How nice for you. And when did you meet her?"

"In September."

"Right after I left? And you didn't see fit to tell me about her. Even though we talked several times between August and December?"

He went to the picnic table and sat on the table, putting his feet on the seat. "Why are you mad at me? Because I didn't tell you? Or because I'm with someone? Because it seems to me you were trying to find me a perfect wife last summer."

She started to respond, then turned away from him when she felt the tears in her eyes. She didn't want to cry in front of him. She didn't want him to know just how upset she was over the fact he was engaged.

"I thought we were friends. And friends tell each other when they get engaged."

Skyler got to his feet and went to her, putting his hands on her arms. "Abby."

She turned around and looked at him. "She's all wrong for you."

He smiled, which made her mad, but also made her realize how much she missed him. "How do you know that?"

She swiped at a tear on her cheek. "Because I googled her."

Skyler laughed. "I'm sorry I didn't tell you."

She put her arms around him and hugged him. "I'm sorry I got mad."

He stepped back and looked at her. "Rebecca and I may not have what your brothers call fireworks in our relationship. But we're good together. She understands the politics of coming from a wealthy ranch family."

Abby studied him for a moment. "Since when do you care about the politics?"

"We all have to grow up at some point and accept our place in the world."

She moved back away from him as she felt her anger rising again. "Your place in the world? Now you sound like your father."

"I'm sorry you don't get it. Your family isn't like mine or the Greenwoods."

"Oh, I get it. You sold out. What happened to that guy who came back from Harvard? The one I hung out with at the gala and who agreed with me it was elitist and snobby. That we were like prized processions being paraded around by our parents."

"Abby."

She shook her head. "Congratulations. You've become a Fremont." She headed for the path, then stopped and turned back to him. "And the fireworks are everything. Why would you want to spend your life with someone who didn't make you feel like you're standing in the middle of a Fourth of July celebration?"

She turned back around and headed down the path. He didn't follow her, which she was glad about. She'd had enough of Skyler Fremont for now.

When Tobias spotted Abby coming back alone from the pond, he nudged Deacon.

"What do you think?"

Deacon watched her as she briskly walked right past them without so much as a glance in their direction, as she headed for the house. "I think you better go make sure she didn't push him into the pond."

Tobias nodded. "Poor bastard."

He left the training pen and walked to the pond. He found Skyler throwing rocks into the water. Skyler glanced at Tobias as he came up.

Tobias picked up a rock and skipped it across the water. "Just wanted to make sure my sister didn't coldcock you."

"Only verbally."

Tobias laughed. "She's a pistol."

Skyler went to the table and sat on the bench. "I figured she might be a little miffed I didn't tell her. But she's like really pissed."

Tobias looked at him for a minute. "Are you in love with this Rebecca Greenwood?"

Skyler scowled. "What kind of question is that?"

"A simple one. You either are or you aren't."

"We're engaged. I asked her to marry me."

Tobias shook his head. "That doesn't answer my question. If you asked me if I love Gemma. I would've answered you before you even finished asking."

"There are different kinds of love."

"No man. There's not. You either love the woman or you don't. And if you don't, then why the hell are you marrying her?" He went and sat next to Skyler. "I'm pretty sure you've been in love with my sister since the gala right after you got home from school."

Skyler sighed. "I thought I was for a while. But not anymore. She doesn't feel the same, so I moved on."

"Marrying someone you don't love isn't moving on. That's just...stupid. And I know stupid. I'm the King of Stupid. Especially when it comes to love. Or at least I used to be."

"So, what are you saying?"

"I'm saying take a step back and make sure you really want to marry Miss Greenwood. And that you're marrying her for the right reasons. If you don't love her, you're headed for a lifetime of misery. That's assuming the marriage lasts, which it won't. Not if you're going into it for any other reason besides love."

"I haven't even married her yet, and you have us getting divorced."

Tobias stood. "Okay. I just have one more question for you. Do you want to be your mom and dad? Because that's where you'll end up if you marry Rebecca. The Skyler who came back from Harvard didn't want anything to do with his parents."

"Aren't you Carmichaels all about family loyalty?"

"To a point. But we're also the first one to point it out when one of us is being an idiot."

Skyler watched Tobias walk away. Why couldn't he answer the question about whether he loved Rebecca or not? Of course, he loved her. These passionate Carmichaels didn't understand that sometimes love is more understated. It's... *Shit.*

Rebecca could be sweet, and she was smart. She was...a Greenwood. He looked up at the sky. She was boring and a bit pretentious. She hadn't been on a horse in years, and would rather spend time at her condo in Dallas, than at the ranch.

He got to his feet. So what if she wasn't fun and adventurous like Abby? It didn't matter that he didn't miss her when they were apart, or even think about her that much. He can't let himself be influenced by Abby or Tobias. They didn't understand. He was the only son, and he had a responsibility to marry the right girl. Rebecca was the right girl. He was sure of it. Or at least he was until he saw Abby on the street. Beautiful Abby.

He headed down the path. "Damn Carmichaels."

Chapter Four

"Insta...what?"

Abby and Tobias headed across the field on Aladdin and Chance, and after a few minutes, she glanced at him.

"I don't want to talk about it."

"I figured as much when you went storming by us a while ago."

She was quiet for a moment, then said, "I just don't get it."

Tobias smiled. "What don't you get, Abby?"

"Why do I care so much about what he does? Let him go marry that woman." She looked at Tobias. "Well?"

"Sorry. I thought we weren't talking about it."

"Well, obviously, we are. I think maybe I like Skyler more than I want to admit."

Tobias took a moment to answer, as though he was considering his options. "Um...what makes you say that?"

She glanced at him. "I thought Deacon was the diplomat of the family."

He shrugged. "I'm trying to evolve."

Abby laughed. "Well, right now I need my crazy brother who doesn't hold back and tells me exactly what he thinks."

"Okay. I think that's true. You like Skyler more than you let on. And you always have. I'm just not sure why you haven't acted on it."

Now it was her turn to take a moment to consider. "I think I didn't want to like him because of who he is and what he represents. From the moment Mother brought him to me at the gala, I rejected any deeper feelings for him because he represented the perfect man for me to marry." She stopped Aladdin. "That's really stupid, right?"

Tobias shrugged as he stopped Chance. "I get it, sort of. But you know our family doesn't think like that. Even Mother didn't think like that. It would've been hypocritical of her. She was far from the perfect match for Dad. We Carmichaels marry for love, not status."

"I know. And Mother was playing the hostess that night. It just hit me wrong, and I was never able to get past it. The really dumb thing is Skyler has always agreed with me. That's why I don't understand why he's marrying Rebecca Greenwood."

"Maybe because he lost his comrade-in-arms. You went away to college. Sometimes it's hard to stand up to the man when you're standing all alone."

She looked at him. "When did you get to be so deep?"

"I've always been deep. I just chose to keep it buried most of the time. But living with a really smart woman has made me up my game a little."

"Speaking of your really smart woman, I'm so glad it all worked out for you. Both you and Deacon found your fireworks person."

"Do you think Skyler is yours?"

"I don't know. I've never kissed him. Would you and my brothers have a problem with that?"

Tobias started Chance moving again. "No. Skyler has proven himself to be a good man. He's respectful, and he's always treated you good. We wouldn't have a problem with you and Skyler as long as he gets his head out of his ass and starts thinking straight."

"Would you finally put the Harvard Yale rivalry to rest?"

"No. Never. We'll always hold that against him."

Abby laughed. "Fair enough." She sighed. "So at the risk of sounding like Deacon, how do I fix this?"

"I'm not sure. But you need to tread softly. If you keep going at him like an...angry she-wolf, you'll chase him right to the altar. He's libel to elope just to spite you."

"Oh, no. That'll never happen."

"How do you know?"

"Social media. She posts everything on Instagram."

"Insta...what?"

"You're so out of it. It's like the new Facebook. Sort of. Her feed is full of venues and cakes. Dresses. Reception ideas. This woman is planning the wedding of the year."

"Yikes. Poor Skyler."

Abby smiled. "Will you help me save him?"

"I'd be a terrible friend and brother if I didn't."

They arrived at Tobias' house and Abby was impressed. It'd been mostly done before she left for college in the fall, but winter set in soon after and they couldn't do much. At Christmastime when she saw it again, there was a foot of snow on the ground. But now, the exterior was finished, complete with flowerbeds, a small grove of apple trees, a chicken coop, a small barn for Chance, and a covered parking space for their vehicles.

"Wow. This is amazing."

"It's great, isn't it?" He rode to a large section on the edge of the meadow that was plowed and fenced in. "This is Gemma's garden. And we finished the greenhouse right before it was time to start the plants."

Abby got off of Aladdin and tied him to a tree, then headed for the greenhouse. "Show me what she's planted."

The greenhouse was beautiful and big. Abby figured about five hundred square feet. It was built with two-by-fours that had been painted green, with panels of glass on the roof and all four sides. The bottom three feet of the walls were stained glass depicting a variety of wildflowers, butterflies, and birds.

"Oh my gosh, it's gorgeous. Who did the glass work."

"Tom Withers. The same guy that did the windows in the new church."

"The new church built thirty years ago?"

Tobias shrugged. "The newer church."

He dismounted, and they went inside. The sun coming through the stained glass fell in rainbows on the three rows of tables covered with starter plants. Abby looked at them all. "Wow. Gemma is really embracing country life."

"Apparently, she loves it."

"This is amazing. Tell her I'd love to help when it comes time to plant them in the garden."

"I'm sure she'd welcome the help. Does this mean you're not going back to school?"

She turned to him. "Deacon didn't tell you?"

"I knew that's what you were talking about last night, but he didn't say anything this morning, so I wasn't sure how it went."

"I'm not going back to school. Ever. I'm home to stay."

"That's great news."

"I know. I'll be here to help Cassidy and the baby. I'll be here to help with Riley if you need it."

"And you'll be here to fix the Skyler problem."

"Yes. My number one priority." She looked at Tobias for a moment. "Am I going to be in the way at the house?"

"Of course not."

She picked up a strawberry plant and looked at it. "It's different now that they're married and have a baby coming."

"Nonsense. They love that you're there. Tanner is still there and will be until fall."

"What if they need room for more babies?"

"Well, they haven't had this one yet. Besides, they turned my room into a giant nursery. Haven't you seen it yet?"

She set the plant down. "No. This Skyler thing has me all distracted. I'll do better about being present for Cassidy. I know she has Gemma, but still."

"Help me water these plants. We'll be staying in the guest rooms until the baby is born." He turned on the water, then looked at her. "You know. It might be too soon to think about this, but you could move into Mother's suite. That'd give Deacon and Cassidy the upstairs to themselves."

"Except for Tanner. "

"Right."

"It's not a bad idea. I don't know though. It might be weird."

"Just think about it. It's more room than you have upstairs."

Abby sighed. "I'm still having trouble believing she's gone."

"I know. Me too."

"But she's happy now, right?"

"Yeah. She's with Dad. For the first time in eleven years, she's happy."

Deacon had a restless night. He wasn't looking forward to the ride in the morning to take his mother's ashes to the oak tree. He could tell the sun was coming up by the way the soft light was hitting the east window. He rolled over to put his hand on Cassidy's stomach, and she put her hand over his.

When she let out a little moan, he raised onto an elbow and looked at her.

"What's wrong?"

"I've been having very mild contractions."

"They're not mild if they make you groan."

She glanced at him. "It's just false labor."

"Are you sure?"

"Yeah."

He laid back down and nuzzled her neck. A few minutes later, she tensed up, and he felt her stomach get hard.

"Whoa. That feels serious." He rubbed her stomach until the contraction passed. "Honey, are you in labor?"

"I don't think so. They're really irregular and they don't hurt nearly enough."

"Maybe I should postpone the ride."

She squeezed his hand. "No. I don't want you to do that. If you did and I really was in labor, then who knows when you'd get to go."

"It doesn't matter when we go. We can go in a month."

"I know. But it's been planned. Everyone has prepared themselves for it. You need to go. Otherwise, it'll be hanging over your heads."

He shook his head. "I'm not so sure."

"It's okay. Really. If this is early labor, it'll be hours before I deliver. You'll be back in plenty of time. Gemma and Ruthie are here with me. I'll be fine." When he didn't answer, she rolled onto her back and looked at him. "Deacon?"

"Right. I'll go. But we're not going to dawdle. I'll only be gone three hours at the most."

"That's fine. Nothing is going to happen in three hours."

He kissed her stomach. "Okay, little girl. Don't come before I get back."

He needed to get up soon, but he closed his eyes for a moment. The next thing he remembered was Cassidy shaking him awake.

"We overslept. It's almost nine."

Deacon sat up. "Shit." He put his hand on her stomach. "Anymore contractions?"

"One or two. Like I said. Very irregular and nothing to worry about."

He kissed her, then got up. "Okay." He went to the window and looked down at the barn. Tobias, Tanner, and Abby were all there, along with Pastor Joe's car. He was there delivering and giving a final blessing to Faith's ashes. "Dammit. The pastor is here."

"It's fine. Tobias can handle it. Just get dressed and go downstairs."

"Right." He put on his clothes, then sat on the bed and put on his boots. He stood and went to Cassidy. "Three hours."

"Okay."

He kissed her, then headed for the door. On the way out, he grabbed his hat.

Cassidy called out after him. "Love you."

He looked back through the door. "Love you. Both of you."

He headed downstairs and Ruthie came out of the kitchen with a cup of coffee. He took it from her.

"Thank you."

"I don't suppose you'll take a minute to eat?"

"Got to go. I'm late. I'll eat when I get back." He held up the cup. "This will hold me. Can you keep an eye on Cassidy? She's been having some contractions this morning. She's says it's nothing to worry about. But…"

"Don't you worry. Miss Gemma and I will keep close tabs on her."

"Thank you."

He went out the front door, took a couple gulps of coffee, then set the cup down on the rail. He jogged down the steps and across the yard to the barn.

Pastor Joe was getting into his car, but stopped when he saw Deacon. "Good morning, Deacon."

"Pastor Joe. Sorry I overslept."

"No worries. Tobias has your mother's ashes."

Deacon shook with him. "Thank you for bringing them out."

"Take care and God bless you all." He got into his car and drove away with a wave.

Deacon looked at the others. "Sorry. I was up most of the night. Then I finally fell asleep as the sun was coming up."

Tobias nodded. "It's fine. Are you ready? We're all saddled up."

"I'm ready."

Tobias handed Deacon the urn with the ashes, and he tucked it into his saddlebag. Then they all mounted their horses and headed out across the field.

Tobias pulled up next to Deacon. "Is everything okay? You seem stressed."

"We're going to bury our mother's ashes."

"I know. But you seemed stressed beyond that."

Deacon sighed. "It's Cassidy. She was having some contractions this morning. She's says it's nothing to worry about. But this is new to both of us. She hasn't been through it. She can't truly know if it's nothing to worry about."

"Well, Gemma's there. And she has been through it. But in any case, we'll get this done and get you back to your wife."

Deacon nodded. "I'd appreciate it."

Chapter Five

"Men are so disgusting."

When Cassidy heard a knock on the door, she called out, "Come in."

Gemma came through the door with a smile. "Hey. I heard you've been having some contractions." She went to the bed and sat next to Cassidy.

"Yeah. I'm not too worried about them yet." As she said it, she got hit with another. Only this one was much more painful and lasted longer. She tried to breathe through it as Gemma took her hand. "Okay, that one worried me a little." She refused to believe she was in labor. As much as she wanted it to be over. She didn't want anything to start until Deacon was back home. Then baby girl Carmichael could do whatever she wanted.

Gemma patted Cassidy's hand. "That was a real contraction. I'm going to sit here with you and we'll see if it was a fluke, or if it was the start of something."

Cassidy nodded. She was really happy Gemma was there with her. Having her friend around all the time had been a blessing. She took a deep breath as she felt herself getting emotional.

"Damn hormones."

Gemma gave her a reassuring smile. "I know exactly how you feel. When I went in to labor with Riley, I was terrified."

"Yeah. Well, you were alone. I have this wonderful family around me. I have you here, holding my hand." She thought about her mother for a moment. Her parents hadn't come to her wedding. And now they'd probably never see their grandchild. They refused to come to Connelly and she refused to play their game and go to them.

"Speaking of family. I have some news to share with you. Something I haven't even told Tobias."

Cassidy was happy to have something else to think about, and she was pretty sure what Gemma was going to say. She smiled. "You're pregnant?"

Gemma laughed. "Takes one to know one. I suspected for a couple of weeks. I took the test yesterday."

Cassidy sat up and hugged her. "Oh my gosh, that's the best news ever. I love that our babies will be so close in age." She laid back down as another contraction hit. Like the last one, it was powerful. She looked at Gemma. "Wow. This is getting serious."

Gemma patted her hand. "I believe you're in labor."

When she could talk, Cassidy said, "I believe you're right." She had a brief moment of panic. But then a calm came over her. She was ready and she could do this. But not without Deacon.

"We've still got lots of time, right? For Deacon to get here."

"Of course." Gemma got to her feet. "I'll call the doctor and have him meet us in Taylorville."

"Wait. I don't want to leave without Deacon. We'll go when he gets back."

"He can meet us there. They should be heading back soon. After the next contraction, I'll go talk to Ruthie and have her find someone to ride out and meet them. Then he'll be right behind us."

"You can go. I'm fine."

"Are you sure?"

"Yes. Go send someone for Deacon." Gemma headed for the door. "But, wait." Gemma turned back. "Why haven't you told Tobias?"

"I think he has enough on his mind right now with Faith's passing, Abby coming home, and you having this baby."

"Don't wait too long."

"I won't." She headed out the door.

Cassidy watched her leave, then took a breath. "April seventeenth. Happy Birthday, baby."

They had arrived at the old oak tree where they'd buried their father eleven years ago. Deacon took the urn from his saddlebag and carried it to the tree as the others joined him.

"We love you, Mother, and hope you're finally at peace in the arms of Clint Carmichael. I know he's happy to welcome you home." Deacon was struggling with losing his mother. The last few years had been hard and he now hated himself for all the times he was frustrated or felt overwhelmed caring for her. He could've been more patient with her. More understanding. Was he wrong to leave her alone so much? Should he have tried to get her more help?

Abby started crying, and he put his arm around her.

Tanner cleared his throat as he removed his hat and spun it around a few times in his hands. "Do you think there are horses in heaven?"

Tobias nodded. "I think everyone has their own version of heaven. There are surely horses in Dad's heaven. Maybe a couple of broncs to ride. Tough bastards that give him a good ride, but don't buck him off."

Abby smiled and wiped away a tear. "And when he wins the belt buckle, it's given to him by the beautiful rodeo queen he fell in love with the first time he saw her."

Deacon knelt and put the urn in the hole Tanner dug in the roots of the old tree. He covered it, then patted the ground before setting a flat rock over it. He stood and touched the heart carved into the tree thirty-five years ago the day Clint asked Faith to marry him.

"Rest in peace, Mother."

When Gemma returned to the room, Cassidy was coming from the bathroom. She leaned on the door frame.

"My water just broke." The calm she was feeling, was now touched with a little panic again.

Gemma went to her. "Oh, honey. Come sit." She helped her to the bed as another contraction hit.

When it passed, Cassidy said, "They're coming really fast and really hard."

Gemma took out her cellphone. "I'm going to call Dr. Hart back." She went into the hall. When she returned, she looked at Cassidy. "He's on his way."

"To Taylorville?"

"No, here."

"Here?" No more calm. Just pure panic.

"He wants to check you before you get in the car and make an hour's drive to the hospital."

"Are you telling me I might have this baby right here? At home?"

Gemma seemed like she didn't want to answer the question. But then she nodded. "It's a possibility."

Cassidy felt another contraction coming. "I need Deacon here. Now."

Gemma helped her breath through the contraction. "Hank's on his way. He'll intercept them. He knows exactly the route they take."

Cassidy nodded. "When will the doctor be here?"

"Fifteen minutes."

It was going to be a really long fifteen minutes. She looked around the room. This was not the plan.

Abby and her brothers were about half-way back when they spotted a rider coming fast toward them. They all stopped as Hank approached and pulled up right in front of them, then looked at Deacon.

"Mr. Carmichael."

"What's wrong, Hank?"

"It's the missus. She needs you back at the ranch as soon as possible."

Deacon looked at the others, then took off at a gallop.

Abby watched him go, then gave Hank a smile. "Thank you, Hank."

"Of course. Miss Ruthie said ride like the devil, so I did."

Tobias nodded. "We appreciate it. Take it slow on the way back and give your horse a rest." He looked at Tanner and Abby. "We don't need to gallop back, but we should probably pick up the pace.

The three of them took off across the field at a lope. When they got to the ranch, Deacon's horse was standing in front of the barn, and they all dismounted. When Abby saw Skyler standing in front of his car near the front porch, she handed her reins to Tanner and crossed the grass to the house.

"What are you doing here?"

"I brought Dr. Hart out. I passed him on the road with a flat."

"Oh my gosh. Thank you."

"So, baby's coming, huh?"

"Yeah. I'm not sure why the doctor is here, though. They should be on their way to Taylorville."

Abby went onto the porch, but before she could open the door, Ruthie stepped out with Riley. "The house is off-limits until further notice."

"Is she having the baby here? Now?"

"Seems that way. Our little girl decided to come, and she's coming with a vengeance, just like a Carmichael."

Abby glanced over her shoulder at Skyler. "But I have to...use the bathroom."

Ruthie folded her arms across her chest. "Deacon said no one comes in. So, no one comes in. Take this young man with you."

Abby took Riley's hand. "Fine."

"You can use the bathroom in the barn."

Abby groaned. "So gross."

She took Riley off the porch and Skyler smiled.

Abby frowned at him. "What?"

"Nothing."

She headed for the barn with Riley in tow and Skyler beside her. They met Tobias coming across the yard.

"What's going on?"

Abby stopped in front of him. "Cassidy is having the baby."

"Why aren't they on the way to the hospital?"

"The baby is coming right now."

"Shit."

"Yeah." She glanced back at the house. "So, Deacon has banished us all until it's over."

"But, I have to pee."

"Join the club. I'm on my way to use the gross bathroom in the barn."

Tobias laughed. "Must be an emergency. I'll just go find a tree." He took Riley's hand. "How about you? Do you have to pee?" Riley nodded. "Okay. We'll find two trees."

Abby shook her head. "Men are so disgusting."

Skyler laughed. "Maybe. But I bet you're a little bit jealous you can't use a tree instead of the cowhand's bathroom."

She sighed. "Maybe slightly."

They continued to the barn and met Tanner coming out the door. "What's going on?"

Abby looked at Skyler. "Can you please...?"

"Of course."

When Abby came out of the bathroom, she found Skyler petting Pale Rider.

"Where's my brother?"

"He went to join Tobias and Riley."

"He had to pee, too?"

Skyler laughed. "No. They headed for the pond." He ran a hand down Pale Rider's nose. "Is this Deacon's new jumper?"

"That's the plan. They've been working with him. But Deacon's been a bit distracted, Tobias is still forbidden to jump by his live-in physical therapist, and as good as Tanner is with cow ponies, he lacks the finesse it takes to jump a horse properly." She looked at Skyler. "I don't suppose you'd have time to come show them how it's done? I'd hate for the horse to learn bad habits from Tanner."

"Actually, I'd love that."

Abby smiled. "Cool. I'll let them know." She definitely wouldn't mind having Skyler hanging around the ranch. She sat on a bench and he left the horse and sat next to her.

"So, how long are you home for?"

"Forever. I'm not going back."

He turned on the seat and looked at her. "You dropped out?"

"Yep."

"Deacon let you?"

She frowned. "I'm twenty-two. I don't need Deacon telling me what I can and can't do." Skyler cocked his head at her, and she sighed. "Deacon is fine with it. Last fall, he told me I needed to give it one more year."

"And you did."

"Yes. I would've stayed until the end of the semester. But after...well, this is where I belong. The family needs me."

"And you need them."

"Yes. I do." She glanced at him. "Especially since my friend is getting married and I won't be able to hang out with him anymore."

"We can still hang out, Abby."

"Promise?"

"Yeah."

She stood and walked a few feet away, then turned toward him. "So, at the risk of sounding like a stalker, I checked out Rebecca's Instagram page."

Skyler rolled his eyes. "Yeah."

"Looks like she's planning a big, fancy wedding."

"I'm leaving it in her hands. I don't really care one way or the other."

"Sure you do." Abby leaned against a stall. "If it was up to you, how would you want to get married?"

He shrugged. "The two of us standing in a field with our horses. Just family around. Although I wouldn't really care if my family was there or not."

Abby smiled. "Skyler...?"

He looked at her for a moment. "What?"

She shook her head. "Nothing. I don't want to start something with you."

"Good. Because I don't want to start something with you, either. I much prefer the Abby who isn't yelling at me."

She laughed, then turned away from him as she tried to hold off the tears that were suddenly in her eyes. He stood and came up behind her, then put his hands on her arms.

"Abby."

She turned around and hugged him. "Sorry. It's been a day. My emotions are all over the place."

He rubbed her back. "I know."

She looked at him. "I'm glad you're here."

"I'm glad I'm here, too."

She laid her head on his shoulder as she fought the urge to beg him not to marry Rebecca. He didn't love her. He couldn't. Not the way he just looked at her. And not the way he was holding her. She had to fix this without pushing him right into Rebecca's arms.

She looked at him again. "I just want to say one thing."

"What's that?"

"My idea of the perfect wedding is just like yours. Only, I'd definitely want my family there."

Chapter Six

"What can I say? Us Harvard guys got it going on."

Deacon sat on the edge of the bed, holding his newborn daughter. He couldn't quite believe she was real. He also couldn't believe how much he loved her. He looked at Cassidy.

"I swear, if anyone ever messes with her, I'll rip their head off."

"I wondered when Papa Bear was going to show up." She put a hand on the baby's head. "It's time to tell her what her name is."

Deacon nodded, then took a breath. "Thea Isobel Carmichael. Welcome to the world." He handed the baby to Cassidy, then stood. "I guess you really meant it when you said you were due."

She smiled. "She and I were both done with the whole pregnancy thing."

"Four hours start to finish. Impressive. I damn near didn't make it back in time."

"But you did."

"And you were amazing."

"It was over so quick, I really didn't have time to think about it."

"Alright. Give me that baby back. I'm going to go introduce her to her family."

Cassidy handed him Thea. "Don't be gone too long."

"We'll be right back."

Deacon carried Thea down the stairs and was met by Gemma and Ruthie, who was wiping her eyes with the corner of her apron.

"Precious angel."

"Where's everyone else?"

Gemma laughed. "Ruthie banished them. They're on the porch."

"Well, bring them in. I want them to meet her."

Ruthie went to the door. "What are you all doing? Get in here and meet your niece."

Abby, Tanner, and Tobias headed inside while Skyler hung back. Ruthie frowned at him. "Don't just stand there. The doctor never would've made it if you hadn't happened by in that fancy car of yours."

Skyler nodded and followed the others inside.

Deacon handed the baby to Abby. "Meet Thea Isobel."

Abby kissed her head. "She's precious. I'm afraid I'm going to break her."

Tobias smiled at the baby, then grinned at Deacon. "Congratulations, pop."

"Thanks."

Tanner touched Thea's hand. "She's so small."

Dr. Hart came out of the kitchen. "I estimate she's about six and a half pounds. We'll weigh her tomorrow when you bring her to the clinic."

Deacon shook his hand. "Thank you."

"My pleasure. I'm glad it all worked out. That was a fast one." He looked at Skyler. "Thank you, young man, for getting me here so quickly. You definitely got my heart going taking a couple of those curves."

Skyler laughed. "I didn't want to be the reason you didn't get here in time."

Dr. Hart waved to everyone. "I'll get out of your hair now. My grandson is coming to pick me up."

"Thanks again, Doc." Deacon went to Skyler and shook his hand. "I think you became an honorary uncle today. Come take a closer look."

Skyler went to Abby and admired the baby. "Wow. I've never been this close to a brand new baby. Not one with two legs, anyway."

Abby looked at him. "She's really sweet, isn't she?"

He nodded. "Yeah. She certainly is."

Thea started to fuss, and Abby squealed, then handed her back to Deacon. "I think she wants her mom."

Deacon looked at them all. "This isn't what we planned for. But I can't imagine a better way to bring this little one into the world." He blinked back a few tears. "Okay. I'm gonna go before the both of us start crying."

Abby watched him carry the baby upstairs. "Oh my God, Deacon's a dad."

Tobias laughed. "You just figured that out? It's been coming for nine months now."

"I know. But it's really real." She wiped her eyes and took Skyler's arm. "Come on, Uncle Skyler, let's go raid the kitchen."

Ruthie ran ahead of them. "Hold on. Don't go rooting around my kitchen. I'll fix you whatever you want."

Tobias patted Tanner on the back. "Hey, Thea's other two uncles are hungry, too."

Ruthie stopped at the kitchen door. "Go sit in the dining room. I'll bring you out some sandwiches."

Abby laughed. "Thank you, Ruthie."

They all went to the dining room and sat down. Abby sighed as she leaned back in her chair. It had started out as a sad day, but had turned into a day to celebrate. Little Thea had showed up to remind them all that life goes on.

"I wonder if Deacon ever ate. He missed breakfast."

Tobias shook his head. "I'm guessing he's not thinking about his stomach right now."

Gemma and Riley came in and joined them. "Deacon may not be thinking about his stomach, but Riley and I are."

Riley rubbed his stomach. "Yeah. I'm starved." He sat on one side of Tobias and Gemma sat on the other.

Tobias took out his phone and checked the time. "How the hell is it only one-thirty?"

Gemma put her arm around him and kissed his cheek. "It's been a very busy five hours since you left this morning."

"I'll say." He looked at Skyler. "So, Uncle Skyler, huh? It took me twenty-eight years in this family to become an uncle."

Skyler shrugged. "What can I say? Us Harvard guys got it going on."

Tobias pointed toward the door. "Out."

Abby put her arm through Skyler's. "No. He stays. He saved the day."

"Hmm. Whatever."

Skyler glanced at Abby, then looked at Tobias. "Abby tells me you've been working with Pale Rider on some jumps."

"Yeah. It's been a little slow going with our rider preoccupied with the impending birth of his child."

"I can imagine. If you need help, I'm pretty available."

Tobias rubbed his chin. "Maybe."

Abby laughed. "Maybe? He's won the Starlight Gala Equestrian Show the last two years. He's a national champion."

"I suppose that's a pretty good reference."

Skyler nodded. "I'll admit, I'll never be as good as you were."

"Water under the bridge, kid. We'd welcome your help." Tobias winked at Abby and she gave him a tiny nod.

After they ate, Abby walked Skyler to his car. "Thanks again for getting Dr. Hart here."

"I'm sure if I didn't happen along, someone else would've."

"But you did. So thank you."

"You're welcome." He looked at the ground for a moment. "How'd it go this morning? Did you finish what you set out to do before Deacon had to leave?"

"Yes. We were on our way back. It's sweet of you to ask."

"I know the woman I saw in public and the woman she was at home were two different people. But I always respected her. When she came up to me at the gala two years ago and told me I had to meet her daughter, she wasn't about to take no for an answer."

"I'm glad you didn't say no. Although, you pretty much said you didn't want to dance with me. If I remember correctly, you said, 'Let's get this over with.'"

"I didn't."

She laughed. "Oh, yes. You did."

"Sorry about that. I really didn't want to be there." He smiled at her. "And neither did you. You had your mind on the barn dance the next night."

"Don't remind me."

"I heard Butch got some girl pregnant and took off when her father threaten to remove his manhood."

"Oh my gosh. I guess I didn't cause any permanent damage then."

Skyler laughed. "Man, that was the best. Of course, you ruined my attempt to step in and save you."

"Just what were you going to do?"

He shrugged. "I don't know. I figured I'd let the situation dictate the appropriate action." He looked at her for a moment. "I better go. I just ran into town for some wine for dinner tonight with the Greenwoods."

"Whoops." She took his hand. "Thank you for being here today."

"I'm glad I was."

"I'll see you around, Uncle Skyler."

He grinned. "I like the sound of that." He got into his car, then waved before driving away.

Abby watched him go. They were back to being Abby and Skyler. At least for the day. She liked that. She missed him. And she more determined than ever to knock some sense into his head about Rebecca. She headed into the house and found Gemma in the living room with Thea.

"Did you steal her away?"

Gemma smiled. "Yeah. I wanted to let Cassidy and Deacon get some sleep." She looked at Abby. "Do you want to hold her?"

"It's kind of scary."

"I know. They feel so small and fragile. But, they're pretty tough." Abby sat next to Gemma and she handed the baby to her. "There you go. You're a natural."

"I don't know about that."

"So, Tobias told me about Skyler being engaged."

Abby groaned. "So stupid. He doesn't love her. I know that for a fact."

"Well, then you can't let him marry her."

"That's the plan. I just don't know how successful I'll be."

"All you need to do is to be Abby Carmichael. He'll remember who he really wants to be with."

"I hope you're right."

"Well, from my experience. You Carmichaels always get what you want."

Abby touched her hand. "Well, Tobias certainly did."

"I'll tell you what, that man. He's kind of hard to say no to."

"Okay. TMI!"

On the way home, Skyler couldn't stop thinking about Abby. Her smile, her laugh, the way she got a fire in her gray eyes when she was mad at him. He tried to shake it off. *It's just because she's back and you haven't seen her in a while. Seeing her again is bringing back how you used to feel about her. That's all it is.*

He was still trying to convince himself when he pulled in front of his father's house. As he got out of the car, Rebecca came out the front door and ran down the steps.

"Oh my gosh, you poor thing." She hugged and kissed him. "I'm sorry you got stuck at the Carmichael's all day."

"It was fine. I like the Carmichaels. They made me an honorary uncle." His father had already convinced the Greenwoods that the Carmichaels were the enemy.

"How sweet of them." Her tone didn't quite match her sentiment. "Did you eat? You must be starving."

"They fed me. I'm fine until dinner."

"Did you get the wine?"

"Yes." He opened his trunk and took out a case of wine. "As you requested."

"You're a doll. Thank you. My folks will be here at six."

"Great. Can't wait."

"Darling?"

"Seriously. I'm looking forward to it." Having dinner with the Greenwoods was like having dinner with the Fremonts. Boring and not at all enjoyable. Certainly nothing to look forward to. But at least with the four of them together, they'd entertain each other and hopefully leave him out of it.

"Go put the wine in the kitchen, then come sit out here on the porch with me. You don't need to get dressed for a couple of hours yet."

"Dressed?"

"Of course, silly. You're not wearing your jeans and cowboy boots to dinner with my parents."

"Right. What was I thinking?"

Chapter Seven

"Funny you should say that."

Skyler sat at the dinner table dressed appropriately for dinner with the Greenwoods. He was wearing dress slacks and a shirt with a pullover sweater. He managed to get away with wearing his dress boots and no tie.

He glanced at Rebecca, who was giving him a silent signal to engage in the conversation. But he didn't want to engage. He didn't even want to listen to the talk about capitalizing on the current market trends in the cattle industry. And the rising cost of raising thoroughbreds.

Bruce Greenwood was one of the top horse breeders in the country. The Fremonts had always concentrated on cattle. The two men hoped to combine their talents, which would benefit both of them. It'd be a merger that'd put the Fremont ranch back on top over The

Starlight Ranch. An unwritten part of the deal was the marriage between their children. Both the only heirs to the family's fortune. They'd be groomed to some day take over the two ranching empires.

When Skyler heard his name, he tuned into the conversation.

"Right, son?"

He looked at his father. "I'm sorry. What?"

"I was telling Bruce how after the wedding, I'd like you to go spend a year or so learning the horse breeding business."

"Um…" He glanced at Rebecca. "I'm not so sure I want to do that."

Leo held back a glare and gave his son a cool smile. "Of course you do. If we're going to expand up here, we need to know all of Bruce's secrets." He'd managed to turn it into a joke and everyone laughed. Everyone but Skyler.

The last thing he wanted to do was spend a year at the Rising Sun Stables. He loved horses, but he didn't love the Greenwood's ranch. It was right outside of Dallas. He may as well be living in the city. Which, of course, is where Rebecca would prefer to live. She hated the rural life outside of Connelly. She hated the original ranch house he'd remodeled and was living in.

She patted Skyler's hand. "Don't worry. I'll convince him."

He pulled his hand away and set it in his lap. He made it the rest of the way through dinner, but afterwards, when Leo invited Bruce into his study for Brandy and to throw around some numbers, Skyler excused himself.

"I need to go check on Scotty. He was favoring his right foreleg this morning."

Leo nodded and smile apologetically at Bruce. "The boy loves his horses."

"Or course. Go see to him."

Skyler made his escape and went to the smaller barn, which was used exclusively for the few expensive horses they kept. They were all Skyler's. He had two jumpers and his four polo ponies. The jumpers got regular exercise and Skyler took them to the arena he'd set up with a jumping course. But the polo ponies didn't see much action. The closest polo club was in Taylorville and the members were hobbyists at best. So Skyler rode them, but he hadn't played competitively since he left Harvard, now almost two years ago.

Scotty's foot was fine. Skyler just needed an excuse to get out of the house. He saddled the horse, traded his dress boots for riding boots, and got into the saddle. Lately, it was the only place he felt like himself. Although, today at the Carmichaels, he'd been pretty comfortable.

He rode out of the barn to the arena. He dismounted at the gate and led Scotty inside, then adjusted a few jumps before getting in the saddle again. He rode around the edge of the arena a few times before lining up and running the course. He went over the twelve jumps three times, then circled the arena a few times at a walk to cool Scotty down.

He went back out the gate and headed for the barn, but at the last minute, changed his mind and headed across the field at a trot. When he could no longer see the house, he urged Scotty into a lope. He loved riding at dusk. Everything had a glow to it. Tinted by the colors in the sky as the sun headed for the horizon. The sun was close to sinking below the mountains when he turned back for home, and it was dark by the time he reached the barn. He dismounted and led Scotty into the dark barn, flipping on the lights as he went through the door.

The other horses all looked at him, seemingly disturbed by the light waking them up.

"I'm sorry guys. You can go back to sleep soon."

He unsaddled Scotty and brushed him down. Rebecca would be mad he took off, so he figured why rush inside?

"What do you think, Scotty? Am I an idiot like Abby thinks? Am I settling for something less to please my parents?" The horse nodded his head and Skyler laughed. "I'll tell Abby you agree with her."

Rebecca was on the porch when Skyler went to the house.

"Where have you been?"

"I took Scotty out for a ride."

She folded her arms across her chest. "My parents are only here for a few days."

"I'm sure my parents entertained your parents, just fine."

She relaxed a bit, and patted the cushion next to her. She was sitting on the swing, his grandfather had built. Leo wasn't much for sentimentality. But the swing was one thing he'd hung onto.

Skyler sat next to her, and she took his hand. "I've hardly seen you today."

"I got sidetracked. It wasn't planned."

She took his hand. "I know. I forgive you."

They talked for a while. Mostly, Rebecca talked about the wedding while Skyler half-listened. When it got late, she patted his hand.

"Want to walk me to my bedroom door?"

"I'm going to stay out here for a while."

"Okay. I'll have to kiss you goodnight right here, then." She gave him a hug and a kiss and when she got up and headed for the door, Skyler wondered what it felt like to kiss someone who brought on the fireworks. Maybe he did need that in his life. Spending time with Abby again, made him realize just how bored he was with Rebecca.

The two of them hadn't been intimate. Rebecca was saving it for the wedding night. Skyler was fine with that. Like everything else involving Rebecca, he didn't care much one way or the other. And he suspected she didn't either. They both seemed to be going through the motions.

When he was sure Rebecca was safely tucked in bed, he took out his phone and called Abby.

"Hey, Uncle Skyler. It's kind of late."

"Yeah. Sorry."

"Is everything okay?"

He leaned back in the swing. "I wanted to tell you how glad I am you're home for good."

"Thank you."

He sighed. "Seeing you again has made me wonder if I'm doing the right thing."

"Are you talking about Rebecca?"

"Yeah. She wants to set a date. Which honestly scares the hell out of me."

Abby was quiet for a moment. "Hmm. When?"

"I didn't want to commit. But she's pushing for the late fall. Before the holidays."

"Why are you telling me?"

He ran his hand through his hair. "I don't know. I'm sorry. I'll let you be."

"No. It's okay. Tell me about your night. How was dinner with the Greenwoods?"

"I don't want to talk about it. But I snuck out afterwards and took Scotty around the course a few times."

"How'd he do?"

Talking with her about riding brought a smile to his face. "Great. He's still got it."

"As do you."

He laughed. "Then I took him for a trail ride. Stayed out until dark."

"Nice. By yourself?"

"Yep. Just me and Scotty. I love riding at dusk when the sky is all pink and the birds are settling down for the night."

"Does Rebecca ever go with you?"

"She's not a horsewoman. Which is weird since she grew up on a horse ranch. She never took to it, and her folks didn't push her into it."

"Well, if you ever need someone to ride with. Give me a call. I am a horsewoman."

He laughed. "I know you are, Miss Rodeo Queen."

"Three years in a row."

He smiled. "And you'll never let anyone forget it."

Tobias turned to Gemma and snuggled up to her.

"So, quite a day, today."

"Yes, it was."

He kissed her neck and started caressing her. "This is going to sound weird, but I found you holding Thea to be quite sexy."

Gemma laughed. "Funny you should say that."

"Mmm." He kissed her again.

"Um...there's something I need to tell you."

"Tell me later." As he pulled her in closer, the bedroom door opened.

"Mom?"

Tobias rolled away from Gemma. "Whoa."

Gemma glanced at Tobias, then sat up. "What's wrong, honey?"

Riley came into the room. "I had a dream." He walked to the bed.

"Do you want to talk about it?"

Riley shook his head. "No. Can I sleep with you?"

"Um..."

Tobias rose onto an elbow. "Of course, kid. How about you stay until you fall asleep, then I'll carry you back to your bed?"

Riley climbed into bed and settled down between Tobias and Gemma. Tobias put his arm around him, then reached for Gemma's hand. She squeezed it, then leaned over and kissed him.

"Goodnight, my two handsome men."

"Goodnight, mom." Riley was quiet for a moment and Tobias thought he'd gone to sleep, but then he looked up and said, "Tobias?"

"Yeah."

"Um...never mind."

"It's okay. What's up?"

"I was just wondering if I could call you dad."

Tobias stopped breathing for a moment and couldn't quite put his thoughts into words. He kissed the top of Riley's head to give himself a moment.

"I'd be honored, Riley. Of course. Of course you can call me dad. I just hope I can live up to the title."

Riley hugged him. "Cool."

Tobias glanced at Gemma. Even in the low light, he could see the tears in her eyes. He shook his head and whispered, "Holy shit."

She laughed and nodded her head.

When Tobias woke, the sun was up and Riley was still in bed between him and Gemma. He looked at her and she was awake and smiling at him.

"I fell asleep."

"Yes. You did."

Riley stirred, then sat up and looked at Tobias. "I'm still here."

"You certainly are. I guess I fell asleep right after you did."

Riley crawled to the end of the bed. "Can I go watch a movie?"

Gemma sighed. "You can watch part of a movie. It goes off when we come out to eat breakfast."

"Okay!"

He ran off and Gemma laid her head on Tobias' chest. "How are you doing this morning, Dad?"

"He laughed. A bit overwhelmed, still." He looked at her. "It's okay with you, right? The dad thing?"

"Of course. In fact, if I'm not being too presumptuous. I'd love for you to adopt him, if that's something you'd like to do."

"Make him a Carmichael? Absolutely." He looked at her. "But that'd still leave you a Stone."

She nodded.

"You were going to tell me something last night. What was it?"

She sat and picked up a pillow, then hugged it to her chest. "I do have something to tell you." She took another moment. "I'm pregnant."

He stared at her for a moment. "You're what? Wait. You're... We're going to have a baby?"

She nodded again. "I know we haven't really—"

He sat up and kissed her. "Good Lord. I don't know if my heart can take much more good news. That's fantastic."

"Really?"

"Yes. Of course. Shit. When?"

"I'm barely pregnant. I figure probably January."

He laid back down. "Don't you think it's about time you said yes to me? Do you really want to be the only Stone in a family of Carmichaels?"

She shook her head. "No. I don't."

"So?" Was she really ready to say yes?

"Well, at the risk of giving you a happiness heart attack. Yes."

He took a deep breath. "It's about damn time."

She tossed the pillow aside and laid down next to him.

He put his arm around her. "So, how invested is Riley in that movie out there?"

"Not invested enough. We'll celebrate tonight."

"Yeah, well, that didn't work out so well last night." He kissed her forehead. "How do people with several kids ever find the time to...celebrate?"

"Well, the fact they have several kids is proof they figure it out somehow."

"I guess you're right. Tonight it is. Unless you want to join me in the shower."

"Tonight, Tobias."

"Right. Okay. I sure am glad you walked into that bar in Malady Springs. Both times."

"What would you have said to me if you'd made it all the way to Austin?"

"Pretty much the same thing I said to you in the bar. Quit screwing around and get your ass back to the Starlight Ranch."

"I would've liked to hear that speech."

"Well, I'm glad I didn't have to give it." He kissed her again. "So, when do you want to do the wedding thing?"

Gemma laughed. "Hmm. How about May first?"

He leaned back and looked at her. "That's in two weeks."

"Too soon?"

"Hell no. I asked you six months ago."

"I just want it to be the three of us. Your family, of course. My parents. If you want anyone else, that's fine, too."

"No. That sounds perfect. So I'm finally going to meet your parents. On our wedding day."

"No pressure."

Tobias sighed. "Shit."

Chapter Eight

"Don't look at me. I don't even have a boyfriend."

Abby came to breakfast late again, and Tobias looked at her.

"The only one who has an excuse to be late to breakfast is Cassidy, yet she's here."

Cassidy smiled and held up a baby monitor. "Until the baby cries."

Abby sat next to Tanner. "Sorry. I was up late."

Tobias raised an eyebrow. "Doing what?"

"None of your business." She and Skyler had talked until almost two. They talked about everything except Rebecca and the wedding. It was wonderful. And she felt like she had her friend back. But it was more than that. She was now sure that he wasn't in love with Rebecca. And more importantly, that he knew it.

"Now you have to tell me."

Deacon reached for a second piece of ham. "Leave her alone, Tobias."

"Fine." He took Gemma's hand. "Now that everyone is here, I need you all to not make any plans for Saturday, May first."

Deacon shook his head. "I've got a meeting in Amarillo. Day trip."

"Cancel it."

"What? Why? What's going on?"

Tobias looked at Gemma. "Because I need you to be at our wedding."

Deacon leaned forward in his seat. "Your what now?"

"Gemma and I are getting married on May first."

Tanner started laughing and Abby stared at him in disbelief. "In two weeks?"

"Yep. Fifteen days."

Cassidy got up and went to Gemma. "Oh, my gosh. Congratulations." She hugged her, then Tobias. "When did this happen?"

"Last night."

Deacon set down his fork, then called out, "Ruthie?"

She came into the room, wiping her eyes. "I heard. I'll get the champagne."

Abby still couldn't quite believe it. "Two weeks?"

Tobias nodded. "We figured, why wait?"

"How are you going to pull off a wedding that quick?"

Gemma smiled. "Well, I'll need some help. But it's going to be very simple. And we're going to do it on our back deck around four when the wild horses come out."

Abby patted her heart. "Okay. That's perfect." It was the type of wedding she'd always pictured for herself.

Tobias put his arm around Gemma. "Just family." Ruthie came into the room with a bottle of champagne, a bottle of sparkling cider, and eight glasses. "Which includes you, of course, Ruthie."

She handed the bottles to Deacon, and he filled two glasses with cider, then handed one to Riley and one to Cassidy.

Gemma raised her hand. "I'll take cider too, please."

He looked at her for a moment, then cocked his head at Tobias. "Do you have something else to tell us?"

Tobias grinned. "Oh, yeah. Gemma's pregnant."

Ruthie lost control of her emotions and started sobbing. Deacon handed her a glass of champagne. "Drink that down, Ruthie. Then I'll refill it for the toast."

Ruthie drained the glass, then handed it back to Deacon. "A whole new generation of Carmichaels." She looked at Abby, who shook her head.

"Don't look at me. I don't even have a boyfriend."

Deacon filled the rest of the glasses. "Okay." He raised his glass. "We have several things to celebrate. Thea. Your wedding. The next little Carmichael. And Abby's homecoming."

Tobias raised a hand. "One more." He looked at Riley. "Riley is going to be a Carmichael too. We're going to start adoption proceedings right after the wedding."

Riley stood up and lifted his cider. "He's going to be my dad."

Everyone raised their glasses and took a drink.

Abby was overwhelmed by all the good news, but she was feeling a little guilty about feeling so happy the day after they buried their mother.

Tanner seemed to pick up on it and he nudged her. "Mother would be really happy about all of this. Her two oldest sons married. Three grandchildren. I'm sure she and Dad are smiling down on us right now."

Abby took his hand. "Thank you, Tanner."

He nodded. "We're all thinking it."

*****

Since Cassidy needed to stay home with the baby, Abby and Gemma went to Taylorville on Wednesday. It was the biggest town near them without going all the way to Amarillo. They spent the morning trying to find dresses for the three of them. The only thing they found was a perfect dress for Thea.

They were at a restaurant taking a break before hitting more stores.

Gemma leaned back in her chair. "I'm never going to find a dress. How about I wear jeans and a T-shirt?"

"I'm sure Tobias would be fine with that. But you might regret it down the road."

"Maybe." It just seems the only place we haven't hit is the thrift store."

Abby pointed at her. "That's not a bad idea."

"I'm not buying my dress at a thrift store."

"I know. But there's an antique store down the street that sometimes has vintage clothing."

Gemma shrugged. "Isn't that pretty much the same thing?"

"No. It's not old unwanted clothing. It's vintage, meaning cool and unique."

"Okay. What do I have to lose?"

"And if you found something vintage, then we could go back to the very first store we went to this morning, and get those two dresses we liked for Cassidy and me. They had a vintage feel to them, with a modern twist."

"I'm glad you came with me, Abby. I'm just a physical therapist. I don't know about any of this. I did like those dresses, though."

"I'm not an expert. But when you've been to as many formal parties as I have, you start to pick up a thing or two. I think those dresses were the same color as the one we got for Thea."

"Oh, my gosh. You're right."

"It's a sign."

"Antique store, here we come."

They finished eating, then went to the antique store. When they told the clerk what they were after, she smiled.

"You're in luck. I had some stuff come in this week I haven't put out yet. It's all been cleaned, but I've been doing some research to figure out how to price the items. Would you like to take a look?"

Gemma nodded. "Yes, please."

They followed the woman into the backroom to a small clothing rack with five dresses hanging on it. "So, you're looking for a wedding dress?"

"Yes. I'm getting married on the first."

"Wow. Last minute on the dress shopping."

Abby laughed. "Well, they just decided to get married three days ago. Not a lot of warning."

"Oh, my."

"Once I finally said yes, we didn't see any reason to wait."

The clerk smiled. "That's so romantic."

Abby put a hand on Gemma's arm. "That's my brother. Mr. Romantic."

"I think I have just the thing." She pulled a dress off the rack. "This belonged to Mabel Armstrong. She was a member of one of our founding families. These garments were recently found in her attic when her house was being renovated. The local museum took some of the things, but they couldn't take it all." She held up the dress. "It's not a wedding dress, but it sounds like it might be perfect for your impromptu ceremony."

Gemma put a hand to her mouth. The dress was from the twenties which hugged the body through the bust and hips, then opened up to a mermaid style skirt. It was a dusty rose satin with beige lace trim over the fitted part. And the skirt was made of layers of beige chiffon over a pink base. It was beautiful and perfect.

Abby shook her head. "Gemma, it's gorgeous. And the color. Those champagne colored dresses would go perfectly with it."

The clerk smiled. "Why don't you try it on?"

"I don't know. I wasn't thinking of anything this fancy. How much is it?"

Abby took the dress from the clerk. "Try it on. You're marrying a Carmichael. It doesn't matter how much it is. And if you love it, then who cares if it's not what you had in mind when we left this morning."

The clerk looked at her. "The Carmichaels out of Connelly?"

"Yes. I'm Abby Carmichael. Gemma is marrying my brother, Tobias."

"I know your mother. Faith, right?"

"Yes."

"We went to school together. I knew her when she met your father."

Abby couldn't believe it. "Oh my gosh, that's incredible."

"How's your mother?"

Abby looked at the floor for a moment. "She recently passed." Word hadn't yet gotten out past Connelly.

"Oh, I'm so sorry."

"Thank you." She looked at Gemma. "Go try it on."

Gemma nodded. "Okay."

As Gemma headed for a dressing room, the clerk smiled at Abby. "Your mother was such a firecracker. She was fearless. Riding those horses. I rode a little myself, but she was a star. And your father. When she met him. Well, there was no doubt they'd end up together."

Abby nodded. "They were very much in love." When she heard Gemma gasp, she went to the dressing room door. "Everything okay?" Gemma opened the door and Abby took a step back. "Gemma, it's—"

"I know."

The clerk wiped her eyes. "You have to get married in that dress."

"I believe you're right." She looked down at the dress. "Even if I will be standing on our wooden deck, outside, at dusk." She looked at herself in the mirror. "So, how much is it?"

The clerk took a moment. "I'll tell you what. Faith was a patron of the historical society. She supported us financially, and she often volunteered at our fundraising functions. If you two ladies promise to continue to support us in her stead, then the dress is my gift to you."

Abby and Gemma were overwhelmed by the generous offer. "I couldn't possibly."

"Yes. You can. Please take it. Wear it well. Pass it down to your daughter someday. The only thing I ask is that you send me some pictures of you and your husband on your wedding day so I can put them up in the shop."

Abby hugged the clerk. "Of course we'll send you pictures. And we'll be there for you. We have a sister-in-law too, so the three of us will take over for my mother. You can count on our support."

The clerk clapped her hands. "Wonderful. I'm Polly, by the way. Polly Simpson." She stood back and looked at the dress on Gemma. "Let me call Sarah. She's our seamstress. Let's make this dress fit you perfectly for your wedding day."

When Abby and Gemma got home, they spotted the men in the training pen with Pale Rider. Skyler was riding the horse around three basic jumps, getting him used to them. Abby went to them while Gemma went inside to relieve Ruthie's babysitting duties.

Tobias smiled at Abby. "How'd it go?"

"It was a success."

"I'm going to go say hi." He looked at Skyler. "I'll be right back."

"Take your time."

Abby climbed up on the fence and sat next to Tanner. "How's he doing?"

"Skyler or the horse?"

"Both."

Skyler rode up to the fence. "I was just about to see if he'll take the first jump."

"Cool. I want to see."

He nodded, then took Pale Rider around the ring a few times, then lined him up and headed for the first jump. The horse took it without hesitation, and Skyler headed for the second one. Pale Rider cleared it and the third one. Skyler came back to Tanner and Abby, then stopped and patted the horse's neck.

"Good job, buddy." He smiled at Abby. "He's a natural."

Tanner shook his head. "I've been working with him for two months and haven't been able to get him to jump."

"I'm guessing the horse picked up on your fear."

"I'm not afraid."

"No. Sorry. Wrong word. Your hesitancy. Jumping horses and riding broncs are two very different things. And honestly, I'd never get on the back of a bronc."

Tanner smiled. "Okay. I get what you mean."

"But what you've done with him is great. He handles well, he's not afraid. You got him to this point. I just got him to the next step."

Tanner nodded. "Deacon will be pleased to hear his jumper is actually jumping."

Abby smiled at Skyler. "Can I take him over a jump?"

"Have you jumped before?"

"You know I have. You've chased the hounds with me. If I can take a rodeo horse over a tree in the field, I think I can handle a two-foot-high jump in an arena."

"Alright." Skyler got down from Pale Rider, then held onto him while Abby mounted him.

She looked down at her jeans and tennis shoes. "I'm not exactly dressed for it. But I don't suppose Pale Rider will care too much."

Skyler laughed, as he adjusted the stirrups. "He won't mind at all. Just be careful in the stirrups, without a heel to keep your foot from slipping.

Abby circled the pen a few times, then cleared the first jump. Tanner whistled and Skyler clapped.

"Take him over the next one."

Abby nodded and headed for the second jump. Pale Rider cleared it. And Abby glanced at the men before taking the third jump. She stopped Pale Rider, then walked him back to Skyler.

She shrugged. "So what's all the fuss about jumping?"

Tanner shook his head. "Shut up."

Skyler took Pale Rider's bridle. "That was impressive, Abby. Quite impressive."

She smiled at him. "Thank you. It was fun."

"If you like, I can coach you a little. Show you how to do it right?"

"Excuse me?"

"Your form could use a little work." He grinned. "Not a lot."

"Okay. Fine. I'd like that. Deacon's getting too old to be the family jumper, anyway."

"Excuse me?"

She looked toward the sound of Deacon's voice. "Oh, hey. Just kidding. You're a champ, brother."

He pointed at her. "Too old? I'll show you too old. Get down from there. Skyler raise those rails a notch."

"Okay. You got it."

Skyler raised the three jumps four inches, then returned to the fence and sat next to Abby and Tanner, while Deacon mounted Pale Rider. He circled the pen, then took all three jumps in succession. When he came up to the fence, Abby jumped down and bowed to him.

"I stand corrected. You're the Carmichael family jumper."

Deacon laughed. "I'll never be as good as Tobias was. And, of course, Skyler here is far superior to me." He dismounted. "I just wanted to show you I'm not too old. Not yet, anyway. But if you want to learn to do it right, with Skyler's help, I'll share Pale Rider with you. Or get you your own jumper. Whatever you want."

Abby hugged him. "You're currently my favorite brother."

Tanner jumped to the ground. "Wow. Give a girl a horse and she forgets about everyone else in the world."

Abby hugged Tanner. "You're my favorite little brother."

"Okay. I can live with that."

Chapter Nine

"So, that must've been fun for you."

Abby went to the Fremont ranch on Friday for a jumping lesson from Skyler. He was waiting out front for her and he seemed happy to see her when she got out of her SUV. He had a light blue shirt on, which was the same color as his eyes. She loved him in blue. With a hat on, he looked like a cowboy. But without it, with his blond hair and blue eyes, he looked he'd be quite comfortable on a beach with a surf board under his arm.

He gave her a grin. "Are you ready for this?"

Abby smiled. "I'm excited and a little scared to get on your fancy champion horse."

"She's just a horse. Nothing you can't handle."

They walked to the arena where Skyler's horse, Penny, was saddled and ready. Abby went to the horse and looked into her eyes.

"You're not going to throw me off now, are you?"

Penny grunted and nodded her head.

Skyler laughed. "Be nice, Penny. Abby's my friend." He glanced at Abby. "Let's get you up on her back and see how you feel."

Abby nodded and mounted Penny. She was a big and powerful horse and Abby could feel her excitement. "She's so..."

"Raring to go? She loves to jump. She gets excited."

"I think she's more ready than I am."

"Just take it slow. Circle the arena a few times and get used to how she moves before you attempt to jump her. I put you on her instead of Scotty because he's a little too set in his ways. He won't cooperate for anyone but me."

"Sounds a bit like Esmeralda. She's never really bonded with anyone after Tobias stopped riding her."

"Go ahead. Just take it slow at first."

Abby urged Penny into a trot, then moved her into a lope as she got more comfortable. She circled the arena several times, then stopped Penny in front of Skyler.

He smiled at her. "Are you ready?"

"I think so."

"Okay. She's a lot different from Pale Rider. She knows what she's doing, and she has no fear. So once you head for the jump, let her have her head. She'll take it from there."

Abby took a deep breath. "Okay. Here goes."

"You've got it."

Abby circled the arena one more time, then lined Penny up for the first jump. The horse flew over it and the next two, then Abby veered away from the course and returned to Skyler.

"Oh, my gosh. She was flying."

"You should've kept going."

"I know. I got scared. She was..." Abby shook her head. "That was amazing. No wonder you love it so much."

Skyler patted Penny. "I want you to run the whole course now. When you approach the jump, lean forward a little and put all your weight on the stirrups. You'll get a smoother landing."

Abby nodded. "Okay. Here we go."

She circled the arena, then ran the full course. Penny cleared every jump, and Abby was exhilarated when she got back to Skyler.

She dismounted and hugged him. "That was so much fun."

He held her embrace. "You're a natural."

When they heard, "What's going on here?" They stepped apart and turned to see Rebecca. She gave Abby a cool smile. "If I'd known jumping lessons involved a hug from the coach, I might've tried it myself."

"I was just excited. I don't generally hug my coaches."

"Good to know." She looked at Skyler. "My folks are getting ready to leave."

"Oh, right. I'll be there in a minute."

Rebecca nodded, then turned and walked away.

Abby gave him a little smile. "Sorry."

He shrugged. "Nothing to be sorry about. Get back up there. I want to see you do it again."

"Don't you have to go say goodbye to your future parents-in-law?"

"I'll go in a minute. Mount up."

Abby took Penny through the course again, then rode to Skyler. "How was that?"

He grinned. "Perfect. You two look really good together." He glanced toward the house when he heard the Greenwoods going to their car. "I've got to go say goodbye. I'll be right back. Then I'll take Penny around and give you some pointers."

"Sounds good."

He sighed, then headed for his parents and the Greenwoods. Abby watched as Rebecca put an arm around Skyler's waist, then glance toward her. Abby looked away. *Whatever, bitch.* She patted Penny, then trotted her around the edge of the arena. "What are we going to do about Miss Greenwood?" Penny snorted. "I know. I totally agree."

Skyler returned five minutes later and gave Abby a smile. "Sorry about that."

"At least it was a goodbye and not a hello."

He laughed. "You got that right." He went into the arena. "Okay. Let's switch places."

Abby got down and Skyler mounted Penny. He spent the next thirty minutes showing Abby different techniques, and she couldn't get over how beautiful Skyler and Penny looked together. They moved like they were one in perfect harmony. And he certainly wore his breeches and riding boots well. She almost preferred it over jeans and cowboy boots.

When he rode back to her and dismounted, she shook her head. "I'll never be that good. You two are connected."

He patted Penny's neck. "Well, we've been at it for a while."

"I could sit here and watch you all day."

He laughed. "Oh no. It's your turn again."

They spent another two hours with Penny, then Abby helped Skyler brush her down and put her in her stall.

Abby leaned on the gate and watched Penny eat some hay. "That was awesome." She turned toward Skyler. "It's exciting running rodeo events. But this is...exhilarating. I love it. It's less frantic and more beautiful."

"I totally agree. That's why I never did rodeo. I found this and never wanted to do anything else." He walked to the stall of one of his Polo ponies. "Although, I love Polo, too. Now that's exciting and frantic, and loads of fun."

"Maybe you can teach me Polo next."

He turned to her. "I can teach you a few things. But we need a few more players to actually have a match."

"No Polo around here?"

"Nothing close. Maybe you could talk your brothers and your sisters-in-law into playing. That'd give us seven players. Three on a team. One alternate."

"I'm not sure if they'd go for that. Actually Gemma and Cassidy probably would. They're pretty adventurous. But, you know polo is..."

"Not rodeo?"

"Yeah. It's a shame though, that you can't play." They left the barn and headed for her car. "I can't thank you enough. That was the most fun I've had on a horse in a while."

"You're welcome. You picked it up fast." They reached her car, and he looked at her. "You're a lot like Penny. Fearless."

"I've spent most of my life on a horse."

He shook his head. "No. It's more than that." He looked away from her and took a breath. "So Tobias is getting married."

"Yes. You're still coming, right?"

"Of course. I was surprised he invited me."

"Well, you're an honorary uncle. So that makes you family."

"I guess it does."

She put a hand on his chest. "Hopefully I'll see you before then."

He took her hand for a moment, then let it go. "You can count on it."

Skyler watched Abby drive away until Rebecca came down the steps and put her arm through his

"So that must've been fun for you."

He glanced at her. "Yeah. Spending time with someone who actually appreciates what I do."

She laid her head against his shoulder. "I appreciate your love of horses. I just don't want to be a part of it. It's okay if we have different interests."

He looked at her for a moment. "Is it? I'm not so sure."

She stepped away from him. "What do you mean?"

He shrugged. "Nothing. I need to go feed the horses." He headed for the barn and she called after him.

"Sometimes I wonder if you love those horses more than you love me."

Skyler didn't respond. He often wondered that himself. He arrived at the barn and went to Penny's stall. "So, what do you think? She's pretty good, right?"

While he fed the horses, he thought about what life with Abby would look like. She was unpredictable. And she certainly got mad at him more often than she should. But he liked that about her. He liked everything about her.

When his father came into the barn, Skyler threw the hay to the last horse, then walked over to him. Leo had been quite a horseman at one time. He'd even done some rodeo. But he hadn't been on a horse in years. Not even for pleasure. In fact, Leo hadn't done anything for pleasure for as far back as Skyler could remember.

Leo folded his arms across his chest. "I want to talk to you about that Carmichael girl."

"Her name is Abby, Dad."

"Right. Abby. It seems you spend a fair amount of time with her and her family."

"And what's wrong with that? They're my friends. I know you see them as the enemy, but they're not. The Fremont Carmichael rivalry is all in your head."

"It goes back a lot of years, son. You don't know what happened."

"Then explain it to me. It seems you're holding a grudge against a man who's been dead for eleven years."

"This isn't what I want to talk about. It's you spending time with Abby."

"She's my friend, Dad."

"Hmm. I think it's a bit more than that. You're engaged, Skyler. You're about to join a very influential family. One that will ensure you an empire worthy of passing on to your children."

Skyler shook his head. "Will you ever have enough money? Will you ever be satisfied?"

"Seems you enjoy the perks of the Fremont fortune. You have a barn full of very expensive horses. You drive a damn nice car. You went to the finest school. I think you're being a bit hypocritical."

He sighed. "Maybe I am a hypocrite. But I'd give it all up. I don't need it."

Leo smiled. "Well, if you screw up your relationship with Rebecca. You just might find out what that's like."

Skyler studied his father for a moment. "Are you threatening to disown me if this merger with the Greenwoods doesn't go through? And when you say marriage, that's what you really mean. It's a business deal, plain and simple."

Leo put a hand on Skyler's shoulder. "Call it what you want. Just don't screw it up. Distance yourself from the Carmichaels. Especially, Abby."

Leo turned and walked away, and Skyler dropped onto a bench. "Bastard." He thought about what he'd said to his father. Could he really give it all up? Despite having to put up with his father, he did enjoy the perks of being a Fremont. And someday it would all be his and then he could do what he wanted. But his father wasn't even sixty. He'd be around a while, trying to turn his son into his pretentious bastard clone.

"Not going to happen, Dad. I don't care what you say, I'm going to Tobias' wedding. And I'm going to see Abby again before that." But tonight, he was expected to take Rebecca to Taylorville for dinner. There were restaurants in Connelly. And most of them were pretty good. But she insisted they go to Taylorville. "Drive an hour to go eat at a restaurant." *Loads of fun.*

Chapter Ten

"Adventurous, maybe. Crazy? No."

Abby was getting ready to go down to breakfast when her phone rang. When she saw it was Skyler calling, she got excited. She took a breath before answering.

"Good morning."

"Hi. I hope it's not too early to call."

She dropped onto the bed and picked up her stuffed horse. "No. I'm back on ranch time."

"I was wondering if you'd like to take a trail ride with me today."

"Sure. I'd love to."

"Rebecca and Mom are going to Taylorville and my dad's out of town. So, I'm all alone."

She propped the horse up between two fluffy pillows. "Poor Skyler."

"Actually, happy Skyler."

It seemed she was helping him see what was really important. "Do you want to come here? We could go to the falls. I found out there's a secret spot behind the water."

"That sounds cool. Sure. Do you have a horse I can ride?"

"I think we can find one."

He laughed. "Okay. I'll be there at ten."

"Can't wait." She ended the call and laid back on the bed. *Don't get excited. It's just a trail ride.* She squealed. She couldn't help it. She was excited. She left her room and jogged down the stairs. When she entered the dining room, Tanner, Deacon, and Cassidy were already there.

She sat in her chair. "Darn it. I was up in time. But then I got a phone call."

Ruthie brought breakfast to the table, and Abby took a sip of coffee as she looked at Deacon. "Skyler and I are taking a trail ride today. Can he ride Nutmeg?"

"Of course. But Esmeralda could really use some exercise. Maybe he can ride her."

"Isn't she kind of excitable on the trail?"

"Nothing Skyler can't handle."

Abby nodded. "Okay. And I'll take Aladdin."

"You can take Pale Rider if you want. Get a little more comfortable with each other."

Abby looked at Cassidy. "I'm sorry my brother has totally re-claimed your horse."

She laughed. "It's fine. We'll consider him the family horse. I'll never have the guts to jump him like you guys do."

"Well, thank you." She looked at Deacon. "You need to buy your wife another horse."

"I will buy my wife whatever she wants."

Cassidy put her arm around him. "Can you buy me a good night's sleep? I'd even take six straight uninterrupted hours."

He kissed her. "I'll see what I can do."

Abby cocked her head at Deacon. "Don't tell me you're one of those dads who sleeps through the baby waking up at night."

"No. I'm not. I wake up. But Cassidy has what Thea wants. Nighttime feedings are out of my hands."

Tanner took a bite of scrambled eggs. "We're supposed to have some thunderstorms this afternoon, so keep an eye on the sky."

"We're going to Angel Falls. So we won't be too far away."

"Are you going to check out the secret spot?"

Abby looked at Deacon. "Unless it's a family secret."

He smiled. "No. It's fine. Skyler is almost family. Just don't jump off."

Abby laughed. "I'm not Tobias. And neither is Skyler."

———— ❧❧ ————

Abby had Pale Rider and Esmeralda saddled when Skyler pulled up to the barn. He was driving his truck today instead of his car, which seemed much more appropriate for the ranch.

Abby smiled at him as he got out. "Slumming in the pickup today, I see."

He shrugged. "I'm in cowboy mode."

Abby took in his jeans and cowboy boots, along with his cowboy hat. "You certainly are. I like Skyler the cowboy."

He joined her at the horses. "We're riding the two jumpers?"

"Deacon thought Esmeralda could use some exercise, and that Pale Rider and I should bond a little on the trail."

"Okay. Makes sense." He ran a hand down Esmeralda's neck. "Are you going to be nice to me?" The horse whinnied and stomped her foot. Skyler laughed. "Hmm. Okay. This should be fun." He mounted the horse, who threw her head and took a small hop.

Abby took Esmeralda's halter. "Hey. You behave." She looked at Skyler. "I can switch her out for Nutmeg or Aladdin."

"No. I got this. Esmeralda's not going to get her way today."

Abby mounted Pale Rider, and they headed across the field, as Esmeralda continued to be testy. But after a half-mile she settled down and seemed to accept the fact she was going on a trail ride with this strange rider on her back.

Abby looked at Skyler. "I think she's beginning to like you."

"She just knows I'm not going to take her bullshit."

When they came to a creek, they stopped and looked for a good spot to cross. With the wetter than usual winter they had, it was higher than normal. They followed it a few hundred feet until they found a spot where the water slowed down after a natural formation of rocks running across the creek bed.

Abby stopped at the edge of the water. "This looks good." She glanced at Esmeralda. "She doesn't like the water too much, so be careful."

Skyler laughed. "If I didn't know better, I'd think Deacon sent me out here on Esmeralda to mess with me."

"I promise. It's completely innocent. The jump she fell on with Tobias, when he got hurt, was a water jump. She's been a little timid around water ever since."

"They do have long memories. You go first. She's more likely to want to go join Pale Rider, then leave him behind."

Abby urged her horse into the water and walked across to the other side.

As Skyler predicted, Esmeralda didn't like that her horse friend had crossed without her. Skyler clicked his tongue and gave her a little squeeze and she stepped into the creek. Halfway across, it seemed she changed her mind. She tossed her head and reared up on her hind legs. Skyler managed to stay on and keep her from turning around. He got her back on track and they finished crossing and came up on the other side.

Abby backed Pale Rider a few feet to give Esmeralda room to realize she was safe and on dry land. "Oh my gosh. Are you okay?"

"She tried her hardest to dump me in the creek. But I'm okay."

"I thought for sure you were taking a swim."

"Not today." He looked back at the water. "Of course, we do need to get back across on the way home."

They continued on and headed into a grove of oaks. When Abby saw a fallen tree, she glanced at Skyler. "Do you feel like taking her over a little jump?"

"Seems like that might be pressing my luck, but sure. Why not?"

Abby circled Pale Rider to line him up with the tree, then ran him toward it. He cleared it without any hesitation, and she stopped on the other side and waved at Skyler. He waved back then lined up Esmeralda.

She seemed to sense what was coming, but once Skyler started her running toward the tree, she remembered what she was trained to do and made a clean jump. Skyler patted her neck as he brought her to a stop next to Abby and Pale Rider.

"There you go. Good girl."

They continued on and as they were about to clear the trees, they could hear the sound of the water falling over the rock face that formed Angel Falls. They cleared the trees and saw the falls and the pool of clear water at the base of it.

Abby urged Pale Rider into a trot and took him to the edge of the pool. She dismounted as Skyler came up beside her.

"This place always amazes me."

"I like the fact that it's all ours. Nobody comes here unless they're invited."

Skyler smiled as he got to the ground. "I'm honored to be one of those few people."

They tied the horses to a tree, then Abby headed for the rocks on the left side of the falls and waved at Skyler. "Come on. This is really by invitation only. Even I haven't seen it."

"I'm right behind you."

They climbed up the rocks, slipped between a tree trunk and a boulder, and came out on a ledge that continued behind the falling water. They both stopped when they saw it.

Abby took Skyler's arm. "The guys told me about this, but wow."

"Definitely, wow." He led her along the ledge until they were behind the roaring water. It was loud and Abby put her hands over her ears, while Skyler looked over the edge. "Is this where Tobias jumped from last year?"

"Yes. My crazy brother."

"It doesn't look that far."

Abby sat on the ledge and hung her feet over. They were completely dry except for a fine mist in the air. "Don't even think about it."

"I don't know. Might be fun. Besides, I don't want Tobias to think he's the only one who's got the balls to do it."

Abby reached for his hand. "Sit down. You're not jumping."

Skyler sat down next to her. "We can do it together."

"No thank you."

He leaned forward and looked down at the water again. "Come on. Where's my adventurous Abby?"

"Adventurous, maybe. Crazy? No."

"Chicken."

She nudged him. "Stop. You're not going to shame me into jumping with you."

"Fine. I'm just saying. Tanner was too scared to do it. Deacon was—"

"Too smart."

"Yeah. That's probably true." He looked over, then glanced at her and grinned. "I know you're thinking about it."

She tried to ignore him and the fact she was tempted to do it.

Skyler got to his feet. "Okay. I'm gonna do it."

Abby stood too. "Please don't."

"Come on. We'll go together."

She shook her head, then sighed. She wasn't about to let him go by himself and leave her behind. "Fine."

"Really?"

"Yes. But right now, before I change my mind." He leaned a hand on the rock wall and started removing his boots. "Take your boots off. Let's go."

They both removed their boots and hats, before returning to the edge of the ledge. Skyler took her hand, and looked at her. "You don't have to go if you don't want to."

"Like you'd ever let me live that down."

He turned toward her. "No. I'm serious. Only go if you really want to."

"Stop stalling. If we're going to jump. Then let's go."

"Okay. On three." He took a breath. "One...two—"

She put a hand on his arm. "Wait. Are we going on three or after three?"

"Three and then jump."

"Okay. Start at one again."

He took another breath and squeezed her hand. "One...two...three..." They both leapt off the ledge with Skyler yelling and Abby squealing. Halfway down, she lost her grip on his hand as he fell faster and hit the water a few seconds before she did. Hitting the water was a shock and it felt like they were jumping onto cement. It was also ice cold. When Abby went under, it took her breath away, and she had a full body brain freeze. She came up gasping for air and Skyler grabbed a hold of her.

"I've got you."

She clung to him. "It's so cold. I can't breathe."

"Slow it down. Take deep breaths." He started swimming with his arm around her toward the shallow water. When they could stand, they stumbled to the shore. After crawling the last few feet, they sat in the sandy dirt on the shore of the pool and tried to catch their breathes.

Abby finally regulated her breathing, then looked at Skyler. She wanted to be mad at him for talking her into jumping. But he looked so scared she'd be upset, she had to laugh.

He cocked his head. "You're not going to yell at me?"

She reached for him and gave him a hug. "No. I should. But I'm not going to." She pulled away from him and hugged herself. "I am freezing, however. So maybe you can do something about that."

He looked at a ring of rocks that had been used for fires in the past. "I'll build a fire."

He got up and started gathering some firewood, then pulled a lighter from his pocket. "That's assuming this will still work."

"I don't care if you rub two sticks together. Just get the damn thing going."

He flicked it a few times and produced a small flame. "Good to go." He dropped the pieces of the wood into the pit, then put some smaller sticks, some dry leaves and some moss from a rock. He lit the dry leaves and they caught fire. He blew on it, then watched it for a moment, before stashing the lighter.

He looked at Abby. "Oh shit."

"What?"

He patted his back pocket, then pulled his cellphone out of it. He held it up. "God dammit."

Abby started to laugh. When he scowled at her, she tried to stop. "I think that's what you get for convincing me to jump."

"So you are mad at me."

"Just a little." He stuck the phone back in his pocket, then knelt by the fire. He blew on the flame again and the moss caught along with the twigs. "As soon as I get this going, I'll go get our boots and hats."

"Just don't jump again."

"Don't worry. Once was enough."

Chapter Eleven

"Here comes the posse."

When the fire was burning well, Skyler climbed the rocks again to retrieve their boots and hats. Abby stayed by the fire and tried to get warm. It didn't help that the clouds were rolling in and obscuring the sun, dropping the temperature a few degrees. She held her hands near the flames and sat as near as she dared.

When Skyler came back, he was favoring his right foot.

"What happened?"

"Stepped on something. I think I got a splinter."

She watched him limp toward him. "Aww. Want me to take it out?"

"No." He sat and looked at the bottom of his foot.

"Are you sure?"

"Yes." He scowled at his foot, then set it back down. "It's fine."

She held out her hand. "Let me see."

"No. It'll hurt."

Abby laughed. "More than jumping off a thirty-foot cliff?"

He sighed, then stretched his foot toward her. She set it on her knee and examined the point of entry. "Man." She sucked in a breath. "This is brutal."

He tried to take his foot back. "Shut up."

She held onto his ankle. "I'm kidding. I know how much splitters hurt. Do you have a knife with tweezers?"

"No. I have a pocket knife. But it's just a blade. No tweezers, And you're not digging it out with my blade."

Abby set his foot down and went to her saddle. "I've got one." She pulled out a Swiss Army knife. "Deacon insists I take it with me everywhere." She returned to the fire and lifted his foot. "Okay, here we go."

"Be careful."

"Oh, my gosh. You're such a baby." She took out the tweezers, then latched onto the splinter and pulled it out. She set it on her hand and showed it to him. "It's massive."

He scowled again. "You're mean."

"And you're a big fat baby."

He started laughing. "Remind me to never get actually hurt around you."

"Well, if you were actually hurt, then I wouldn't make fun of you."

He looked at the waterfall. "I can't believe you jumped with me."

"I can't believe I did either. But now I'm one up on Tanner and Deacon."

He looked at her. "You're going to tell them?"

"Of course. Why wouldn't I?"

"Because Deacon will assume I talked you into it."

She pointed at him. "You did talk me into it."

He held his hands over the fire. "Fine. Tell them. Brag about it. You earned it."

When they heard thunder, they both looked at the sky. The weather was getting dark and ominous to the east. Abby looked at Skyler. "I think we're going to get rained on."

"Yeah. And if it rains upstream of the creek, it could flash flood. We better get back across it."

They both put their boots on, then Skyler kicked dirt over the fire to put it out. Abby went to the horses and got them ready to ride. Skyler joined her and they mounted up. Esmeralda didn't like the unsettled weather, and she was nervous.

Skyler patted her. "You're okay. It's just a little weather." The horse didn't seem to be convinced. And he was having some trouble keeping her from bolting.

They headed back the way they came, and as they were going through the oaks, it started raining. It started out light, then became a downpour. They found some cover under the branches of an oak tree and stopped the horses.

Abby shook her head. "Good thing we got dried off by the fire."

Skyler laughed. "We're completely soaked again."

"At least the rain isn't as cold as the pond was." She shivered. "At least that's what I'm going to tell myself."

Skyler peered out at the rain. "I'm not sure it's going to end anytime soon." Esmeralda was still nervous, and he tried to calm her. He finally dismounted and tied her to the tree. He talked to her and tried to soothe her. It helped a little. But if she had the chance, she'd take off.

Abby got off of Pale Rider and tied him as far away from Esmeralda as she could and still keep him under the tree. The branches were giving them some protection, but they were still getting wet. The wind picked up, and she was just as cold as she had been after getting out of the pool beneath the waterfall.

Skyler went to her and put his arms around her. "Body heat is all I can offer you."

"I'll take it." She felt warm and safe wrapped in his arms and she laid her head on his chest. He was just the right height at around six-feet, and they fit together perfectly.

They stayed that way for several minutes, but the rain showed no signs of letting up. Abby took a step back. "Another thing Deacon always insists I take with me is a blanket." She went to her saddle and pulled a wool blanket out of her saddle bag. "Sit down. We'll share."

Skyler sat and leaned against the tree, then Abby sat in front of him. He put the blanket over his shoulders, then wrapped his arms and the blanket around her.

Abby glanced back at him. "I'm guessing this is a no no in the fiancé handbook."

"Probably. But it's a matter of survival."

Abby didn't mind at all it was a no no. It was time she faced it. She liked him. She liked him a lot. Now she was more determined than ever to prove to him marrying Rebecca would be a mistake. The way he was holding her. She didn't think it'd take much convincing. He seemed to already be there.

"Skyler?"

"Yeah."

"Thank you for coming with me today."

He laughed. "Are you being facetious?"

"No. I'm serious. You made me realize something."

He rested his chin on her head. "What's that?"

"That we'll always be friends. No matter what. That you'll be there for me if I need you."

He hugged her a little tighter. "To keep you warm?"

"Yes. But also to talk me into doing wild and crazy things. Stuff I'd never do if I weren't with you."

"Well, then. I guess you're welcome."

"When I'm with you, I'm not scared. Whether I'm jumping a horse, or jumping off of a waterfall."

"I'm sure my adventurous Abby would be just as adventurous if I weren't around."

She shook her head. "No. I don't think so."

"Okay. I'll gladly take the credit."

She was quiet for a few minutes, then said, "Skyler?"

"Yeah."

"Do you think it's ever going to stop raining?"

He laughed. "I don't know. And honestly, I don't really care."

"This is kind of nice, isn't it?"

"Yeah. It's kind of nice."

She laid her head back against his chest again, and watched the rain pour around them.

It *was* really nice and there was no one Skyler would rather be caught in a rainstorm with, then Abby. He tried to imagine Rebecca in this situation. But since she'd never get on a horse, they'd never be in this situation. He'd never sit out a rainstorm under a tree with her. Or jump off of a waterfall into freezing water. Rebecca wasn't who he wanted to spend his life with. Tobias was right. If he loved her, he would've been able to answer Tobias' question.

When the rain started to let up, he was disappointed. The rain ending meant his time with Abby was ending. It meant going back home and spending an evening with Rebecca and his mother.

Abby patted his arm. "Looks like it's slowing down."

"Yeah."

She had been leaning against his chest, but she sat up and looked back at him. "My brothers are probably about to send out a search party."

He sighed. "I'm sure. Mom and Rebecca are probably back by now, too."

"Did you tell them you were going for a ride?"

"No. I figured she'd call if she got back before I did."

Abby smiled. "On your soggy phone?"

"Do you have yours?"

"No. I didn't bring it."

"Deacon doesn't insist you have it on you, too?"

"He does. I just forgot to bring it." She got to her feet. "We should go." She held out her hand. "Let me help my poor wounded cowboy to his feet."

He slapped her hand away and stood up unassisted. The rain had almost stopped and Esmeralda had calmed down. He led her out from under the tree. "Okay, girl. Let's get you home to your safe and dry barn."

They both mounted their horses and continued through the trees. But as they got near the creek, they could hear the water rushing. They rode up to it and found it a foot higher and moving way too fast to cross safely with the horses. Especially one who didn't like the water.

"Well, shit."

Abby looked up stream. "We're going to have to follow it to the road and cross over the bridge."

"I think you're right. How far is that?"

Abby shrugged. "Six or seven miles."

He turned Esmeralda toward the road. "Hour. Hour and a half. Not bad."

Abby pulled up beside him. "Then three miles down the road to the ranch."

"I don't suppose you have a snack in your saddlebags."

"I actually thought about bringing a picnic lunch."

"Thought about it, huh? That doesn't fill up my stomach."

They followed the river, heading for the road and the bridge.

About a half-mile upriver, Skyler spotted two horses on the other side of the creek. He and Abby both stopped, and as the riders got closer, they recognized them as Deacon and Tanner.

Skyler laughed. "Here comes the posse."

Abby waved at her brothers and they stopped on the other side of the creek.

She called across the water to them. "We got caught in the downpour. By the time we got to the river, it was too high to cross."

Deacon nodded. "You're okay, though?"

"Yes. Thank you."

"I tried to call you."

"I know. I left my phone at home."

He looked at Skyler. "I tried to call you, too."

Skyler pulled his wet phone out of his pocket. "My phone took a dunk in the waterfall pool."

Tanner looked at Abby, then smiled. "You guys jumped."

Deacon shook his head. "No. These two are too smart for that." He cocked his head. "Right?"

Abby smiled. "Well. We kinda sorta jumped together."

"Dammit, Abby." He scowled at Skyler. "You should know better."

Skyler shrugged. "Sorry. It just kind of happened."

Abby nudged him. "He triple dog dared me."

Deacon sighed and ignored Abby's comment. "Well, if you're okay, we'll head back."

"We're fine. Thank you." Deacon turned his horse and Abby called after him. "Can you have Ruthie fix us something to eat?"

He glanced back at her. "Sure. I imagine all that swimming made you hungry."

Tanner grinned at her. "Now I have to do it."

Deacon looked at him. "Tanner."

Tanner turned his horse, then looked back at Abby and gave her a thumbs up.

Skyler and Abby started riding again, and he looked at her. "I told you Deacon would blame me."

"Don't worry about it."

"Yeah. But now Tanner will do it, to prove he's not afraid. Then he'll break his arm or something, and it'll be my fault."

"You're not responsible for what Tanner does. If he breaks something, it's on him."

They continued following the creek as they headed for the road. After a few minutes, Abby glanced at Skyler. "Can I ask you a really personal question?"

He answered her with a bit of trepidation. "Sure."

"When Rebecca is in town with you at the ranch, does she stay in your house with you?"

"Are you asking if we're sleeping together?"

She sighed. "I guess, yeah. But obviously—"

"No. She doesn't. She stays at the main house."

"Because of your parents?"

"No. Because she wants to wait until we're married."

"Oh. Okay. So she's—"

'No. I don't think she is."

Abby stopped Pale Rider. "Then why?"

He shrugged as he stopped Esmeralda. "I think the better question is, why I don't care one way or the other."

"That is a very good question." She started her horse moving again. "But you've...done it before, right?"

"Yes, Abby."

She was quiet for a few minutes. "Well, to reciprocate you being honest with me and answering my inappropriate questions. I tell you, I haven't. Done it, that is."

Skyler stopped again. "Really?"

She looked at him. "You don't have to sound so shocked."

"I'm not shocked. I'm...surprised I guess." But actually, now that she'd said it. It didn't surprise him at all.

"I'm Abby Carmichael. I have three big, intimidating brothers. No one around here would ever dare touch me. Let alone...*touch* me."

"Right. I know the feeling." He smiled. "But you were in school away from here for three semesters."

"City boys. No thank you." She urged Pale Rider into a trot.

Skyler caught up to her. "Thank you for telling me."

She glanced at him. "Well, you're pretty much the only friend I have. Who else am I going to tell?"

As they approached the road, they saw a familiar truck and horse trailer, parked along the side next to the bridge. Tanner was standing behind the trailer and gave them a wave.

When they reached him, he smiled. "Thought I'd save you the last three miles."

Abby stopped Pale Rider and dismounted. "Thank you. I wasn't looking forward to riding along the road." She glanced at Esmeralda. "Especially with Miss Nervous Nellie."

Skyler got to the ground. "Yeah. I think she's had enough for the day."

They loaded the horses and Tanner began driving toward the ranch. He cranked up the heater and Abby, sitting between the two men, held her hands out to the blast of heat.

"I don't know if I'll ever be warm again." She glanced at Tanner. "Thank you for picking us up."

"No problem. How was the jump?"

Abby glanced at Skyler. "Far and cold."

Skyler laughed. "But damn fun."

"Man. I need to do it now." He looked at Abby. "Will you do it again with me?"

"No. I think once was enough." She nudged Skyler. "Mr. Adventure might, though."

Skyler laughed. "Maybe. But not anytime soon."

When they got to the ranch, Tanner told them he'd put the horses away while they went to eat. They walked across the grass toward the house, and Skyler stopped at his truck. "I should go home."

"You're already late. You might as well eat something."

"I don't know."

"You can use my phone and call to let them know you're okay and will be home soon."

"I do like Ruthie's cooking."

"So, it's settled. You'll stay."

He blew out a breath. "I'll stay."

Chapter Twelve

"Excited, anxious, and a bit terrified."

Skyler decided not to call Rebecca. She was going to be mad, so he'd just as soon save it until he got home. Ruthie served them a great meal, and since it was mid-afternoon, it was only the two of them.

Skyler looked at Abby across the table. "So you must've shut down a few guys in Georgetown."

"Not really. Maybe one." She took a drink of iced tea. "I think he was slightly devastated when I said goodbye to him with such short notice."

"I can imagine."

"Not everyone sees me like you apparently do. I think I was viewed as the quiet girl from the country who didn't party and actually went to class."

He picked up a piece of fried chicken. "Well, I guess that's why you were there."

"And while I was there. You were here, getting engaged."

"Yet here I am with you. Eating fried chicken." He looked at the chicken breast in his hand. "Is this Carmichael chicken?"

"Yes. But I don't like to think about it."

"Why is it different from eating one of your cows?"

"I don't see the cows every day. The chickens are wandering around the yard. I feed the chickens. I gather their eggs."

"Just don't name them. It's a lot easier that way."

"I learned that lesson a long time ago. When I was twelve, I went a whole year without eating chicken when Henrietta ended up on the supper table."

He leaned back in his chair. "I swear, Ruthie is the best cook in northern Texas."

"Yeah. We're lucky to have her. Of course, she's so much more than our cook."

Ruthie came into the dining room. "That's right. I'm the one who had to kill and serve poor Henrietta." She picked up the dirty dishes. "Are you needing dessert?"

Abby shook her head. "No thank you. I'm stuffed.

Skyler smiled at Ruthie. "Me too. Thank you. That was delicious." Ruthie nodded and left the room, while he leaned across the table and lowered his voice. "Does she listen to all of your conversations in here?"

Abby smiled. "I believe so. But it's okay. She's family."

He leaned back again. "I guess I should get going."

Abby gave him a quick smile. "Well, it was quite the day. Thanks for sharing it with me."

"We'll have to do it again soon. But without the high dive and the rainstorm."

"I don't know. I think both of those things were my favorite parts."

He laughed. "Maybe so."

They both stood and Abby walked him to his truck. "I hope Rebecca's not too upset with you."

He shrugged. "Maybe I'll get lucky and beat them home."

They reached the truck and Abby looked at him. "I'm going to say something I shouldn't."

"Go for it. It's never stopped you before."

"You shouldn't have to worry about someone getting mad at you because you were out longer than you expected."

He took her hand for a moment. "I know. Seeing you that day in town has given me a whole new perspective. I just need to figure out how to get out from under the mess I've finally realized I'm in."

"The first step is realizing you're in a mess."

"I guess you're right."

She gave him a quick hug. "I'm here. If you need to talk. Or hide out. Or just get away."

"I know you are, Abby. And that's what will give me something to hold on to." He opened the truck door and got in. "I'll talk to you soon."

"Have a good night."

Abby watched Skyler's truck until she couldn't see it anymore. When she turned to go to the house, she saw Tobias coming from the field with a few of the cowhands. She walked to the barn to meet him.

He dismounted and handed Chance off to one of the men, then gave Abby a smile.

"What's up, Abigale?"

"Nothing. I just came to say hi."

He cocked his head. "Sure you did. Come with me while I walk off his stiff leg." They headed down the path to the pond. "I heard you and Skyler were taking a ride today."

"Yes, we did. We went to the falls and checked out the secret spot."

Tobias glanced at her. "Behind the falls? I thought that was a family secret."

Abby put her arm through his. "Deacon said I could show Skyler."

"Hmm. I guess he's sort of family, being an honorary uncle and all."

"Yeah, it was pretty cool." She gave him a smile. "Especially when we both jumped."

Tobias stopped walking and stepped away from her. "You jumped?"

She grinned. "We both did at the same time."

"Dammit, Abby, you could've gotten hurt."

"We didn't."

He squinted at her, then pulled her in for a hug. "You have guts, little sis." He stepped back again and looked at her. "I'm surprised Skyler did it, though."

"It was his idea." She held up a hand. "He didn't talk me into it. It was my decision."

Tobias laughed. "I don't think anyone could talk you into anything." They started walking again. "So what was his fiancé doing while you two were jumping off waterfalls?"

"I don't want to talk about her. The more I hear about her, the more I see what a sterile relationship it is. He deserves more than that. He deserves to be with someone who makes him happy and enjoys the things he enjoys."

"Like jumping off of waterfalls?"

"Yeah. Stuff like that." And sitting out rainstorms under a tree.

"I'm sure he's beginning to realize that. Otherwise, he wouldn't be spending so much time with you. You coming back might've saved him from a lifetime of misery."

"I'd sure like to think he would've figured it out even if I didn't come home."

"Maybe."

She took his arm again as they continued down the path. "So, now that the news of your new baby has had time to sink in, how do you feel about it?"

"Excited, anxious, and a bit terrified."

"You're a great dad, Tobias. Look how much Riley loves you."

"Well, when you start out with a six-year-old, it's easy. But a newborn? I see Deacon with little Thea, and it scares the shit out of me."

She squeezed his arm. "You'll be fine. I'm sure Deacon had his moments or being terrified over the last nine months."

"Yeah. But the bastard's a damn brick wall. He never shows it."

"That doesn't mean he's not feeling it."

※

Skyler was tempted to pass by the drive to the main house and go to his house to avoid a confrontation with Rebecca. But that would just postpone it. He'd still have to give her an explanation when he did see her. So, he made the turn and drove the two miles to his parent's house. It was the house he grew up in, but it had always felt like it was their house and he was just existing there. Unlike Abby, he loved his time away at Harvard. And when he got back and his grandfather granted the original homestead and the surrounding fifty acres to him, he couldn't wait to make the place his own. He'd been in it almost a year now, and he finally felt like he had a home.

Rebecca called it his cabin and though she'd never come right out and said she'd never live there, she'd made it quite clear it wasn't up to her required standard of living.

He sighed as he approached the house. So many red flags. Why didn't he see them? Why did it take Abby coming home for him to realize what a colossal mistake it'd be to give into his parents' wishes and marry someone he didn't love? He pulled in front of the house and Rebecca came through the front door. She stood on the porch for a moment, then went down the steps and met him at his truck.

He got out and gave her a small smile. "I know. I should've called, but I dropped my phone in some water. It's not working."

She looked at him for a moment. "And no one had a phone around you?"

"You were busy with mom." He felt himself getting irritated. "I shouldn't have to check in with you and give you a play-by-play of my whereabouts."

"It's the considerate thing to do. Where were you?"

He thought about lying to her. But he didn't want to do that. It'd just make things worse. "I went on a trail ride with Abby."

Rebecca scowled and shook her head. "That woman again."

"She's my friend."

"Hmm. And how would you feel if I spent all my time with a guy friend?"

He really wouldn't care all that much. But it would hurt her feelings to tell her that. Even though he didn't love her, he didn't want to hurt her.

"I would trust you."

"I know you have history with this woman. I don't trust her. And I don't trust you with her."

Skyler leaned against his truck. "Rebecca, be honest with yourself for a moment. How upset would you actually be if I was fooling around with someone else?"

"So, you are having an affair?"

"Whoa. That's not what I said." He put a hand on her arm. "I'm not having an affair with Abby. What I said was, would it really matter to you?"

She pulled her arm away. "Of course it would. Are you asking my permission?"

"No. Dammit, Rebecca. You have to admit. We're not madly in love with each other. I don't think you even like me all that much."

"Of course I like you. Or at least I thought I did."

"But do you love me?"

She glared at him. "Are you saying you don't love me?"

"I'm asking you the question. Just answer it."

She huffed, and then turned and walked away from him. He watched her stomp up the steps and go inside the house. "Well, there you have it." *She couldn't answer the damn question.* Just like he couldn't answer it when Tobias had asked him.

He got back in his truck and drove to the main road, then followed it to his driveway. His house was only set back a quarter of a mile. He parked the truck next to his car and went onto the porch. He really wished his phone was working, because he wanted to call Abby. Even though he'd just left her, he missed her already.

He sat on the porch and looked up at the starry sky. It was clear and beautiful. The storm that had hit them early was passed leaving a dark night sky filled with stars. He wondered it Abby was on her porch looking at it too.

Chapter Thirteen

"Don't want to disappoint the horses."

The next morning when Skyler went to the barn to feed his horses, Rebecca came to see him. When he saw her enter the barn, he prepared himself for a fight, but she gave him a smile as she approached.

"Good morning, Skyler."

He looked at her suspiciously. "Rebecca."

"When are we leaving for the farmer's market?"

He looked at her with an arm full of hay. "We're still going?"

"Unless you've made other plans."

He tossed the hay to Penny. "I thought we were fighting." He was a little disappointed that apparently they no longer were.

She walked over to him and took his hand. "I've decided to trust you."

He pulled his hand from hers and took a step away. "We still need to talk about things, Rebecca."

"I know. But not today. Let's go to your quaint farmer's market and do whatever we're supposed to do there. And have a nice day. We'll talk tonight."

Skyler sighed. He really didn't want to spend the day with her. "Okay. Sure. I'll be done here in a half-hour."

"Then you need to change."

He looked at his jeans and western shirt. "I'm not changing. This is fine for an outing in Connelly."

"Okay, fine. Come get me when you're ready."

He watched her leave the barn. She was up to something. He just didn't know what. He turned to Penny. "That was weird, right?"

Penny was too busy eating to give him a response. Rebecca had given up too easily. She liked to milk their arguments for as long as possible. The fact that she decided to trust him, was suspicious.

"Rebecca, I don't believe you."

As they ate their breakfast, Abby smiled at Deacon, Cassidy, and Tanner. "Who wants to go to the farmer's market with me?" When she got no response, she frowned. "Come on, guys." She looked at Cassidy. "You want to go, right?"

"I'd love to. But I don't want to take Thea out in a crowd yet."

"Of course. You've got an excuse." She looked at her brothers. "But you two don't."

Deacon glanced at Cassidy. "I need to stay here and get some work done. And Tanner has school. You're on your own, kid."

"Maybe Gemma will go with me."

"I think she and Tobias are running to Taylorville today to get some stuff for the wedding."

"Man. You guys all suck."

Deacon smiled at her. "Because we're too busy to go to town with you?"

"Yes." She finished her last bite of breakfast. "I'll go by myself."

Tanner got to his feet. "Get some of the Morgan's strawberries."

Deacon nodded. "Yeah. And some rhubarb. Ruthie can make me some rhubarb pie."

"That's so gross." She looked at Cassidy. "Any requests?"

Cassidy thought for a moment. "A jug of apple cider."

Deacon looked at her. "You're still craving that? You're not pregnant anymore."

She shrugged. "Maybe it wasn't because I was pregnant. Maybe I just love apple cider."

Abby stood. "Okay. Strawberries, rhubarb, and apple cider."

Ruthie stepped into the dining room. "I need some jalapenos for dinner tonight. You'll save me a trip to town."

Abby nodded. "And jalapenos."

She went upstairs to get ready. When she went into her room, she found one of the barn cats sitting on her bed. "Patches, what are you doing in the house?"

Patches meowed at her.

"I've got nothing for you." She went to her window and closed it. The screen had fallen out again, and she was waiting for one of the men to come replace it. It seemed every time the wind blew in from a certain direction, the screen would fall out. But she liked to sleep with the cool night air coming in. Patches had taken advantage of the open window and climbed up the big oak tree next to the house.

Abby looked at the tree branch the cat must've used. It was about four feet from the window.

She looked at the cat. "Pretty remarkable break-in. That's an impressive jump. If you'd missed, it would've been quite a fall."

The cat meowed again as Abby grabbed her purse, then picked him up. "You're not staying." She went downstairs and out the front door, then let Patches go on the porch. The cat looked at her for a moment, before running for the barn.

"Go do your job and catch a mouse."

On the way to her car, she saw one of the men. "Russ?"

"Yes, Miss Carmichael?"

"I found Patches in my room. Can you fix the screen today please? It's fallen out again. I like to open the window at night."

"Of course. The wind came in from the east again last night. I'll get that done today, Miss."

"Thank you."

On the way to town, she thought about her day yesterday with Skyler. Jumping from the waterfall. The rainstorm. Even taking the splinter out of his foot. It had been an adventure. She hoped it was the first of many, now that she saw him in a different light. She was definitely ready to ride out of the friend zone. There was just the little matter of his fiancé.

———————✦———————

Rebecca took Skyler's hand. "So what exactly are we looking for here?"

The farmer's market was always busy, and they had to dodge other shoppers while they made their way down the row of booths. "Nothing in particular. But there's a guy who's usually here who sells oat treats."

"Like cookies?"

"Not for me. For the horses." He waved at some people he knew.

"Oh. Of course. Your precious horses."

He still couldn't understand her objection to horses. Her father raised them. She'd been around horses all her life. She spotted something that caught her eye and she pulled him toward a booth.

She picked up a jar of honey. "Now this I'm interested in. I love honey in my tea."

"Local honey. Get a jar."

She smiled at him. "I didn't bring my purse."

He took out his wallet and paid for the honey.

Rebecca squeezed his arm. "Thank you."

When he heard, "Clover honey. Good choice." He turned to see Abby standing behind them.

"Abby."

Rebecca tightened her grip on his arm. "Hello, Abby." She glanced at Skyler with a look that confirmed she didn't really trust him.

Abby nodded to Rebecca, then smiled at Skyler. "I didn't know you liked the farmer's market."

Skyler glanced at Rebecca. "I came for some of those oat treats."

"Oh, yeah. I need to get some of those, too. I think he's down at the end."

"Thanks." It was really good to see her and he hated the fact Rebecca had a death grip on his arm. "What are you shopping for?"

She held up a shopping tote. "Strawberries for Tanner. Rhubarb for Deacon. And jalapenos for Ruthie. I also need a jug of cider for Cassidy. But I'll get that right before I leave."

He loved the fact she was there getting stuff for everyone else. "And what are you getting for yourself?"

"I just might have to get a jar of honey."

Skyler took out his wallet again. "I'll get it for you."

He heard Rebecca sigh.

Abby smiled. "Thank you." He paid for the honey, then handed it to her. "Do you guys want to go visit the horse treat guy with me?"

"Sure." Skyler started walking, and he felt Rebecca hesitate. He glanced at her. "You coming?"

"Of course. Don't want to disappoint the horses."

They found the booth selling the oat treats, and they both bought a dozen of them. When Rebecca nudged him, Skyler looked at her.

"What?"

"I need to use the ladies' room."

"There's a row of outhouses over there."

She looked mortified, and Abby smiled at her. "There's a very nice bathroom in the café. And they don't mind if people use it during the farmer's market."

"Thank you." She looked at Skyler. "Will you walk me there?"

"It's a half-block. I'll wait right here."

Rebecca scowled, then glanced at Abby before walking off.

Abby cocked her head at Skyler. "You probably should've gone with her."

"I didn't want to."

Abby tucked the treats into her bag. "I'm surprised to see you two out and about. I figured she'd be pissed at you today for coming home late."

"She was. Then this morning, she's all smiles. Not sure what's going on."

"She's sensing she's losing you."

"Okay, maybe. But she doesn't even want me."

Abby put a hand on his arm. "She wants what you represent. She wants to make her daddy happy. Marrying Skyler Fremont is a big win. Losing you would be a big blow to her social image."

"That's so stupid."

"I agree." She looked at him. "So, what are you going to do about it?"

"I'm going to tell her it's over. I just need to do it in a way that doesn't get me into too much trouble with the old man." If that was possible, which he really doubted.

Abby shook her head. "I really hate your father."

"Join the club. There are actually quite a few members." He leaned in close to her. "I had a really good time yesterday."

She smiled. "Me too."

He moved a step closer. "Abby, I..." He stopped when he saw her look over his shoulder, then took a step back. He turned to see Rebecca approaching. "Did you find it okay?"

She shivered. "Yes. Not a whole lot better than the outhouses."

Skyler doubted she'd ever been in an outhouse. And he knew the men's room at the café was fine. He assumed the women's room was too.

She looked at him. "Can we go, now?"

He glanced at Abby. "I guess we're going.'

"Okay. It was nice running into you."

"I'll see you around, Abby."

"Small town. It's inevitable. Enjoy your honey."

When they got to the car and Skyler opened the door, Rebecca glared at him. "Could you be any more obvious?" She mimicked him. "Here Abby, let me buy that for you."

"It was a jar of honey, Rebecca."

She shook her head. "No. It was so much more than that." She got into the car and when he got in behind the wheel, she turned toward him. "We need to go back to Dallas. I'm really tired of this rustic lifestyle of yours. And I'm really tired of *accidentally* running into your *friend.*"

"Do you think I planned that?"

"It wouldn't surprise me."

He shook his head. "I don't want to go to Dallas. I've got a wedding to go to on Saturday."

"One of those Carmichaels?"

"Yes. It's family only, and they invited me."

"So, you'll have Abby all to yourself."

"That's not why I'm going. Tobias is my friend." He started the car and drove out of the parking lot. It was time to have the talk. "Rebecca."

"No. Don't. Not while we're driving down the road."

"When, then?"

"Tonight. After dinner." He just wanted to get it over with. And he was tempted to pull over and just do it. But he didn't. He'd wait until tonight and hopefully do it without too much drama.

<hr>

Skyler kept himself busy all afternoon to make the time go faster. He wanted to have the talk with Rebecca and be done with it. Whatever repercussions came from it, he'd deal with. He spent some time with his horses, then rode out with a couple of the men to check on the herd. He wasn't a hands-on cowboy when it came to the cows. Not like the Carmichaels were. But he liked to ride out a few times a month to stay on top of what was going on with the herd. Since his father didn't ride anymore. It was left to him to be the man in charge in his father's stead. He'd much rather spend his time with horses. He got horses. Cows were impersonal and not very bright.

He got back to the ranch right before dinner and unsaddled his horse. He'd planned on taking a shower, but he got back too late.

When he went into the dining room, his parents and Rebecca were already seated. He sat next to her and she wrinkled her nose.

"You smell like cows."

"Sorry, I got back late."

Rebecca picked at her meal and was quiet. When Helen asked her if she was okay, Rebecca said she had a slight headache. Skyler tried to ignore the warning bells going off. What was she up to? He was determined to get the talk over with.

When dinner was over, Rebecca sighed loudly. "I'm so sorry. I need to go lie down. I believe I'm getting a migraine."

Skyler looked at her. "I'll walk you to your room."

They both stood and Skyler took Rebecca's arm and led her to the stairs. Once there, she pulled her arm away and Skyler followed her up to her room. When they reached her door, he took her arm again.

"I know what you're doing."

"I'm not doing anything, Skyler. I have a headache."

"Delaying the talk won't make me forget about having it."

She squinted and rubbed her temples. "Well, why don't you just tell me right now what's on your mind?"

Skyler sighed, then shook his head. "Not like this. And not in my parent's house."

She gave him a small smile. "Tomorrow. I promise."

Skyler nodded. "Right. Tomorrow." He hated that he was giving into her little game. But he didn't want her making a scene. And she would if he pushed her. He walked away as she closed her bedroom door.

Chapter Fourteen

"No half-shots allowed on my wedding day."

It was wedding day and everyone was expected at Tobias and Gemma's house by four. The ceremony was set to start at four-thirty. They'd kept it small as they planned. The only non-Carmichaels would be Ruthie, Skyler, and Gemma's parents, Tim and Marion Stone.

Tobias paced around the living room and Gemma went to him.

"What's all this? Are you second guessing the whole wedding thing?"

He stopped and hugged her. "God, no. I'm just having a bit of a problem with the whole in-laws thing."

"Relax. They'll love you."

"I'm never been the guy a woman's parents liked. Let alone, loved."

"Well, I'm not just a woman. I'm going to be your wife. And we're not kids. If they have a problem with you, then screw them. They've certainly had their problems with me over the years."

"I don't see how."

She glanced toward Riley's bedroom door. He was playing until his grandparents arrived. She lowered her voice. "Well, I was twenty when I came home from college and told them I was pregnant with a married man's baby."

Tobias grinned. "I guess that's a bigger hurdle to get over than anything I've done. At least anything they'll ever know about."

She put a hand on his chest. "It's going to be fine. They'll love you."

"We're going to keep the news that I also impregnated their daughter under wraps for now, right?"

"Tobias, I already told them."

"Shit."

"It's okay. The fact that you stuck around and you want to marry me gives you quite a few points. Add the fact you want to adopt Riley, and I think you're safe."

He glanced at the front door. "They're late. I should've gone to the end of the road and picked them up."

"My father's driven on a dirt road before. They'll be here soon. And I'm pretty sure riding in a car with them for five miles would be a lot more awkward than meeting them on our front porch."

"I guess you're right."

Riley came running from his room. "When's Grandma and Grandpa going to be here?"

"Any minute, honey." She glanced at Tobias. "Let's go on the porch and wait for them."

The three of them went to the porch and a few minutes later, they heard a car approaching.

Gemma smiled at Tobias. "Take a breath."

He nodded. "I'm fine."

The Stones drove up in a Toyota and parked next to Tobias' truck and Gemma's car. When they got out of the car, Gemma waved. "Hey. You made it."

Her father, Tim, stretched out his back. "That's quite a road you have."

They came onto the porch, and Riley ran to them and hugged them. Then Gemma hugged them both before taking Tobias' arm. "This is Tobias."

He shook hands with Tim. But when he offered his hand to Gemma's mother, Marion, she pulled him in for a hug. "I'd say this occasion calls for a hug."

He nodded. "I believe you're right." He stepped back. "Welcome to the Starlight Ranch. Although, this is just a tiny piece of it."

Tim looked around. "It's beautiful country. Where does your property start?"

"At the road. And then about three hundred square miles of high Texas desert."

"Wow. Impressive."

Gemma took her mother's arm. "Come inside. Let me show you the house."

They all went inside and Gemma gave them the tour, all the while bragging about how Tobias built most of it himself. They ended on the deck, which was decorated for the reception with bouquets of wild flowers, strings of lights, and candles along the railing. Tobias pointed at the meadow.

"If we're lucky, the wild horses will come out just about the time the ceremony is over."

Marion smiled. "It's beautiful. Even without the horses."

"Well, they've been invited, so they better show."

Abby, Cassidy, and the baby arrived at three to help Gemma get ready and they disappeared into the bedroom along with Marion, leaving Tobias alone with Tim. Fortunately Riley was there to act as a buffer.

Tobias wasn't usually at a loss for words, but this was Gemma's father and he had no idea what to say to the man.

When in doubt, offer a drink. "Can I get you a beer? Or I have rum and scotch."

"A beer would be great, thanks."

Tobias looked at Riley. "Beer?"

Riley laughed. "I'm a kid."

"Right. I keep forgetting that. I'm pretty sure we have the fixings for a Roy Rogers."

"Yes!"

"Coming right up."

Tobias managed to keep Tim entertained until he had to leave to get himself and Riley dressed. They went into Riley's room to get ready. In lieu of a suit, Tobias was wearing dark denim jeans, a beige shirt, and a brown leather vest. He was also wearing a dusty rose tie.

He smiled as he tied it. Gemma had shown it to him with trepidation, not sure how he'd feel about wearing it. But he didn't care. He'd wear a pink suit if she asked him to. They were getting married, and that's all that mattered. He looked at Riley, who was dressed just like him. He tied Riley's tie and then put the black cowboy hat on his head.

"Looking good, buddy."

Riley smiled. "We're twins. Except you're not wearing your hat."

"Yeah, I going without one tonight, but other than that, we are. This is the one time maybe my brother won't show up wearing the same thing as me."

They both put on brown boots, then Tobias sent Riley to his grandfather on the porch with a warning to stay clean. Tobias went to the kitchen and poured himself a rum before joining Tim and Riley on the porch.

Tim smiled at him. "I'm assuming my daughter picked your ties?"

Tobias laughed. "Yeah. Apparently, they match her dress."

"Well, you two gentlemen look very nice."

Riley hugged him. "Yeah. Dad and I are twins."

Tim glanced at Tobias, then smiled and gave him a nod. It seemed he was accepted.

Even though she and Cassidy weren't officially standing up for Gemma, they wore the dresses from Taylorville that complimented Gemma's dress. And Thea was wearing a tiny matching dress, as well.

Marion wiped her eyes. "My goodness. Aren't you all beautiful?"

Gemma hugged her. "Thank you, Mom. And thank you for being here."

"Of course, my darling. I'd never miss your wedding day." There were a few years in her life when Gemma wondered if this day would ever come. As a single mother trying to raise Riley and finish her degree, then establish a career, there wasn't a lot of time to date, much less find a husband. Thank goodness, she'd never fully committed to Preston. And double thank goodness she walked into that bar in Malady Springs.

She almost didn't. It wasn't something she did. Especially alone. But something told her to go that night. And there he was. Her handsome cowboy.

She wiped at a tear, and Abby hugged her. "No tears."

"I know. I'm just really, really happy."

Abby smiled at Marion and was hit with a twinge of sadness. Her mother wouldn't be there on her wedding day. Just like she'd missed Deacon's and now Tobias'. But they had each other, and that was more than enough. She left the ladies and went to see how Tobias was doing.

She found him on the back deck with Riley and Tim. She glanced at the drink in Tobias' hand.

"How you doing?"

"I'm good." He held up the drink. "First one of the day. Don't worry."

She patted his arm. "I'm not." She stepped back and admired his outfit. "Very, very handsome."

"As are you."

She laughed. "That's what I was going for."

When they heard a vehicle approaching, they went to the front porch. Deacon arrived with Tanner and Ruthie. As Tobias introduced them to Tim, Pastor Joe drove up with Skyler right behind him.

The pastor got out of his vehicle. "I asked young Skyler to follow me. Your road is still a bit rough, Tobias."

"I know. It's a work in progress."

Abby went to Skyler, who looked very nice in jeans and a leather coat over a dress shirt.

He smiled at her. "Wow. You look beautiful."

"Thank you. So do you. I was half afraid you wouldn't make it."

"I wasn't about to miss this."

"How goes it at the Fremont Ranch?"

"She's been avoiding me. I've barely seen her since the farmer's market."

"So, you haven't had the talk?'

He shook his head. "Not yet. Not for lack of trying, though."

Ruthie went to the back of Deacon's truck as he opened it up. "With all you strong young men around, I shouldn't need to carry any of this."

Tobias grinned at Riley. "I think she's talking about you, kid."

Riley laughed and went to help Ruthie. Tobias, Deacon, and Skyler joined him. And they carried all the food Ruthie had brought. The only thing left was the cake which she'd only allow Deacon to carry.

He frowned at her. "Are you sure you want me to carry it?"

"I trust you not to fall and drop this beautiful cake I spent all day yesterday making."

"Oh. Right. But no pressure."

"Just follow me. I'll clear a path."

Deacon picked up the triple layer cake and followed Ruthie up the porch steps and into the house. When he set it on the table, he took a breath. "Okay. I don't ever want to be responsible for carrying a wedding cake again. Tobias, the next one's on you."

"You got it."

Abby admired the pale yellow cake with a cowboy holding his bride in his arms on top of it. "Where did you find that, Ruthie?"

"I didn't. Gemma found it."

"It's adorable and perfect." She left the kitchen to go let Gemma know everyone was there. Abby came out a few moments later with Cassidy, Thea, and Marion.

Marion smiled at Tim. "You're up, Dad."

He nodded, and everyone else went to the porch. Tobias and Riley stood by Pastor Joe, and the others stood around the porch. Cassidy went to the CD player and started the song Gemma had picked, and

Abby watched Tobias take a breath. When he saw her looking at him, he gave her a wink.

Abby took Skyler's arm when Gemma and her father came through the door. The look on Tobias face brought tears to her eyes, and she dabbed at them. Skyler handed her a handkerchief from his pocket and she hugged his arm.

"She's so beautiful."

Skyler nodded. "Yeah. I think Tobias agrees with that."

Like Deacon's wedding, the ceremony was very short, and just as Pastor Joe was announcing them as husband and wife, the wild stallion came out of the trees. Tobias kissed Gemma and everyone clapped. Then they all went to the deck railing and watched as the rest of the herd came out. Maybe it was Abby's imagination, but it seemed they all looked toward the house for a moment before they started eating.

Skyler put his arm around her waist. "They're beautiful."

She nodded. "They're perfect."

Ruthie got busy in the kitchen getting the meal ready that she'd prepared earlier in the day, while the men set up a long table on the deck for everyone to sit at. Tobias brought out the rum and the scotch and poured a drink for Tim, Deacon, Skyler, and himself. He offered one to Pastor Joe, who was staying for dinner. But he declined and asked for a beer instead.

"Coming right up, Pastor."

When Abby came out with a giant bowl of salad, Tobias asked if she wanted a drink.

"I'll have a half-shot of scotch, please."

Tobias poured her a full shot. "No half-shots allowed on my wedding day."

When they were all seated at the table, Deacon stood and raised his glass. "Just a few weeks shy of a year ago, Tobias was toasting Cassidy and me for our wedding. He brought up a night in Abilene that is still a little foggy for me. But it was a turning point. And my hope that night was that Tobias would have his own turning point. Which he did a few months later. Which brings me to this night." He looked at Tobias. "You owe me."

Tobias laughed. "How so?"

"If I hadn't gotten my head out of my ass and married Cassidy, you never would've met Gemma. Because she never would've been on the road to Connelly and we all know what happened on the road to Connelly."

Tobias stood. "Okay, brother." He glanced at Gemma's parents. "We don't all know what happened on the road to Connelly."

Deacon laughed. "Right. Sorry. But in any case. You're welcome."

Tobias took a drink, then shook his head. "That was the worst toast ever."

"Sorry. I believe the scotch has gone to my head. I've been avoiding alcohol in solidarity with my pregnant and now nursing wife. Well, mostly anyway." He took a drink and sat down.

Cassidy patted his hand. "I believe I'll be driving home tonight."

Tanner stood. "I'd like to say something, even though I don't have a drink in my hand. Both of my brothers have somehow managed to land perfect women. I hope I'll be so lucky when me time comes. Down the road. Like way, way down the road."

Tobias laughed. "We get it kid."

Tanner sat and Abby stood. "Okay. I guess it's my turn. I am a very lucky woman. Not only do I have three frustratingly wonderful brothers, but I have their two wives who I consider sisters. And I'm an aunt of two and counting. I have been blessed by all of you. And..." She swallowed the lump in her throat. "Sorry. I'll end with *Slàinte Mhath!*"

Skyler gave her a hug, then stood up. "I know I'm the only non-family member here, but I'd like to say something if I may?"

Tobias nodded. "Of course."

Skyler cleared is throat, then started singing the Harvard alma mater. Tobias stood and threw a roll at him. Skyler laughed as he dodge the roll.

"Just kidding. I couldn't resist." He held up his glass. "I didn't really know any of you guys until that night at the gala a year and a half ago. I knew about you of course. Who around here doesn't know about the Carmichaels. Tobias was two years ahead of me in school. Abby was two years behind me. Deacon you were just this enigma I was sort of afraid of."

Deacon smiled. "Was?"

"Maybe I still am a little bit. Anyway. Here I am at this very intimate, family only affair and I'm honored to be included. It means more to me than I can say." He held up his glass. "To the bride and groom. May you always have the magic of wild horses in your life."

Chapter Fifteen

"I bet it was the rubber boots."

After dinner, everyone was sitting around talking. When Abby saw Skyler motion for her to join him on the deck, she got up and followed him outside. They stood at the railing and looked at the meadow, lit only by moonlight.

Skyler glanced at Abby. "It's beautiful here. I thought I had privacy, but this is really secluded."

"I'd like to see your house one of these days."

"Yeah. It's pretty cool. Big and rambling. But I like that it's the original homestead my great-grandfather built. There's even an old barn. Which I'm still working on." He leaned over and looked at the steps leading to the grass. "I don't suppose you'd like to take a walk with me. I think there's enough moonlight to see okay."

Abby looked at her heels. "Not really dressed for it." She looked at Skyler. Did she really want to pass up this opportunity to spend some time alone with Skyler? "What the heck?" She took off her shoes and slipped on a pair of rubber boots sitting at the top of the steps. "This will work."

Skyler laughed. "That's what I like about you Abby, you're always up for anything."

She shrugged. "You only live once."

He took her hand, and they went down the steps and came out in knee high grass. Abby lifted her skirt. "Whoops. Didn't take the tall grass into consideration." It was also cooler away from the house. "A bit chilly, too."

Skyler stopped walking. "I'm sorry. We can go back."

"No. It's fine. It's nice." She was looking forward to spending some time alone with him.

He slipped off his jacket. "Well, the least I can do is give you my jacket." He hung it over her shoulders. "Is that better?"

"Yes. Thank you." Skyler had always been a gentleman around her. He was polite. He respected her. And he was really, really handsome. But did he feel about her the way her brothers thought he did? She wasn't sure.

They followed the line of trees along the edge of the meadow where the grass was shorter, and Skyler took her hand again.

"Can I talk to you about something?"

"Of course."

"And I need you to not get mad at me. I just need you to listen."

"Okay." Perhaps she got mad at him a little too often if he has to preface his request with that.

"Rebecca's not a bad person. But she's shallow and spoiled. And we have nothing in common. I've come to the conclusion, a little late maybe, but still. The marriage is basically a business deal between her dad and mine." He took her other hand and held them both, standing less than a foot in front of her. "You know I don't want to marry Rebecca. If you hadn't come back, I might've gone through with it. And I would've been miserable." He let go of one of her hands and touched her face. "Like I told you, I'm going to call it off. I'm doing it for me. But I'd also like it to be for you, too. And not because I'm your friend." He smiled at her. "I need to know how you feel about me, Abby. Because even if you only feel half of what I do—"

Abby put her arms around his neck and kissed him.

"Whoa." He looked at her for a moment, then kissed her back.

Abby whispered, "Did you feel that?"

He cupped her face in his hands. "The fireworks?" She nodded, and he kissed her again.

Abby pulled back, before taking a step away. "Wait."

"What? Why?"

She took a breath. "You're still engaged to Rebecca."

"I don't care about Rebecca." He took a step toward her.

"I know. But she's still currently your fiancé." Abby put a hand on his chest to stop him from kissing her again. "As long as she's your fiancé, we can't do this."

"Abby."

"I'm not going to be the other woman, Skyler."

He shook his head. "You're not the other woman. You're the only woman."

She moved further away from him because she didn't quite trust herself. "Then you need to break up with Rebecca."

"Of course. I've been trying to."

"Try harder. Because until you do, no more fireworks."

Skyler nodded. "Okay. Of course I will. I'll do it tonight. Or first thing in the morning because she'll be in bed by the time I get home. So does this mean you feel the same way I do? The way I've always felt about you?"

"I'd say the fireworks answers that question." She took his hand and started walking again. "What's your dad going to say when you ruin his business deal?"

Skyler sighed. "He'll have a stroke. He'll yell and threaten me. And when I stand firm, he'll probably disown me."

Abby stopped walking again. "You don't mean literally, do you?"

"Yes. I mean literally."

"Skyler. I don't want to be responsible for that."

"It's okay. He'll get over it. Who else is he going to leave the ranch to?"

"No. Skyler. This is serious. You need to think about this. You can't give up everything to be with me. I'm not worth it."

"Of course you are." He touched her cheek again, and smiled. "Besides, you have enough money for both of us."

She laughed. "That's true. But maybe I only like you because you're heir to the Fremont fortune."

"Yeah. That sounds like you. You're all for the elitist snobbery of the Texas Ten."

She hugged him. "Seriously, though. You need to think about it."

"You want me to marry someone I don't love to please my father?"

"No. But I don't want him to disown you, either."

"Well, I do have a trust fund set up by my grandfather that Dad can't touch. The house was also left to me, along with the fifty acres around it. The car's in my name. I own my horses. I'd be okay."

"A trust fund, huh?"

"Yeah. I never wanted to tell you because it made me sound like a snob."

She laughed. "It kind of does."

"You don't need to worry about me. Honestly, it'd be kind of freeing to be out from under his thumb." He looked at her. "Would you not give up your family money for me?"

She tapped a finger to her lips. "Hmm. I don't know." She smiled. "I might have to check out the fireworks again before I can answer that question."

Skyler leaned in and kissed her. "Well."

"Screw the money." She kissed him back, then stopped herself. "No. We can't do this."

"Right. I'm an engaged man."

"We should go back. They're probably wondering where we disappeared to." Kissing Skyler felt too good. And here, alone in the moonlight, it was too tempting to let herself go.

They headed back, following the same path and when they got to the house, Tanner was coming down the steps.

"Oh, there you are."

Abby frowned at him. "We weren't gone that long, were we?"

"No. You just didn't tell anyone you were taking off."

Abby felt herself getting annoyed. "I didn't realize I had to announce my plans to everyone."

Skyler squeezed her hand as he smiled at Tanner. "Sorry. My fault. It was a last-minute decision."

Tanner nodded. "Sure. It's fine. I think everyone is getting ready to leave."

Abby went up the steps and traded the boots for her shoes, then followed Tanner and Skyler into the house.

Gemma smiled. "Thank you everyone for coming. You made our day as special as it could be."

Tobias took her hand. "We'll be leaving for Malady Springs in the morning and be back in a few days."

Deacon smiled. "Take your time. We've got you covered."

They said their goodbyes to everyone, including Riley, who was spending the next few days at the main house. As they all left, Skyler walked Abby to Tanner's truck.

"So, I'll call you tomorrow."

Abby nodded. "Okay. Good luck."

"Thanks. I'm going to need it." He squeezed her hand, then opened the door for her. "See you, Tanner."

Tanner waved. "Thanks for coming."

Tanner pulled out and followed Deacon's Jeep down the road to the highway.

"So, how goes it with Skyler?"

Abby sighed. "Good, I think."

"How good is good?"

"He's been trying to break up with Rebecca, but she knows it's coming and has been avoiding him."

"Whoa. So he's breaking up with her for you?"

"He's breaking up with her because he never should've gotten engaged to her in the first place. It was just like I said. A merger between the two ranches."

"Well, I'm glad he finally figured that out. But where's that leave you two?"

"Well...we kissed."

"You haven't kissed him before?"

"No."

Tanner grinned. "Really?"

"Yeah."

"Cool."

"I guess it's cool. I hope it is. Maybe it was just the moonlight and the fact we were alone."

"I bet it was the rubber boots."

Abby laughed. "They were pretty sexy."

Tanner glanced at her. "The guy's a goner for you. He always has been. You're the only one who never saw it."

"That's what everyone keeps telling me." She looked out the window at the Jeep's taillights. She hoped it was true. Kissing Skyler was wonderful. And so much better than she could've imagined. *Stay strong, Skyler.* She looked at Tanner.

"Cassidy told me a little about what happened with Hallie. I'm sorry."

Tanner shrugged. "I guess it wasn't meant to be."

"She met someone else?"

"Yeah. In San Antonio. She's moving there after graduation and going to school there."

"That sucks."

"I'm over it."

She suspected he probably wasn't. He'd like Hallie all through high school. "What about Hester?"

"What about her?"

"Well, she's always kind of liked you too, right?"

"I don't know. It'd be weird, though. Being Hallie's sister and all."

"Right. Her identical twin sister."

"Like I said, weird."

Abby patted his knee. "There's someone out there for you. You just haven't met her yet."

Tanner laughed. "If Tobias could find someone like Gemma, then I know I have a chance."

Abby laughed. "Now that's weird, right? He's such a child, and she's...not."

"Yeah, well, they really love each other."

"Good for them."

"Abby?"

"No. I mean it. I love Gemma and I love Tobias too, of course. I have three very unique brothers. Deacon, the father figure. Tobias, the class clown." She looked at Tanner. "And you, my sweet little brother."

"I am sweet, aren't I?"

"Now you sound like Tobias."

She was quiet the rest of the way home and she thought about what being with Skyler in this new capacity would be like. She'd barely dated. The boys around here had always bored her. And the college boys were so different. And not in a good way. So, even though she was twenty-two, Skyler would be the first man she'd spend time with. Looking back, she realized, she'd already spent more time with him than any other man whom she wasn't related to.

She looked at Tanner. "I'm pathetic."

"How do you figure?"

"I've barely dated. And when a guy does like me—for a year and a half—I don't even recognize it."

"That doesn't mean you're pathetic. You just weren't ready to see it. The important thing is you do now. And it's not too late."

"Barely. The man's engaged."

"But he's not married."

"Thank God for small favors."

Chapter Sixteen

"Are you absolutely, one hundred percent sure?"

When Skyler pulled up to his house, he saw the glow of a cigarette. There was only one person he knew who smoked and would also be sitting on his porch. He then spotted his father's car and parked next to it. He got out and went up the porch steps.

"Dad."

"Where have you been, son?"

"I'm pretty sure I'm old enough to not have to answer that question."

"That's alright. Because I already know. Rumor around town is, another one of those Carmichael boys got married today."

Skyler leaned against the porch railing trying to stay upwind of the cigarette smoke. "Why ask the question if you already know the answer?"

"Have a seat, son."

"I'd rather stand."

"Rebecca told me tonight you've been reluctant to set a date. She's pretty upset."

Skyler nodded. This wasn't how he pictured telling his father, but he might as well get it over with. "I don't want to marry Rebecca and she knows it. I'm not going to marry her. I've been trying to talk to her for days. But she's been avoiding me because she knows it's coming."

Leo took a final draw from the stub of his cigarette, then flicked the butt into the yard. "You might think about what you just said."

Skyler checked to make sure the butt hit dirt and not something flammable. "I don't need to think about it. I've made up my mind. I think I always knew I couldn't go through with it. You messed with my head, Dad. You made me think it was the right thing to do. It may be the right thing for you. But it's definitely not the right thing for me."

"Do you want to think about that for a moment?"

"No, Dad. I don't. I'm not going to marry Rebecca."

"So you think Miss Carmichael is the answer? That the Carmichaels can offer you an escape from the horrible life you've been force to live."

"That's not what I said. I'm not going to marry Rebecca so you and Bruce can seal your deal. The Carmichaels have nothing to do with that. I don't love her and she doesn't love me."

"So you're choosing them over me. Her over Rebecca."

I'm choosing me, Dad. My happiness. Which is something I thought you would choose for your only son, too."

Leo got to his feet. "You have until next week to get that rickety old barn of yours in shape. I want your horses, and everything you deem is yours, off my property a week from today." He went down the steps and headed for his car without saying anything else.

Skyler watched him go. "Wow. Okay." He sat in a chair. He felt lightheaded and a little sick to his stomach. Not by the fact his father just disowned him. He expected that. But he'd done it so quickly. Without any thought or hesitation. It was cold. Even for Leo Fremont.

Skyler sat for several minutes trying to wrap his head around what had just happened, before taking out the new phone he'd bought and calling Abby.

She answered with, "Hi. I was kind of hoping you'd call."

"Abby."

"What's wrong?"

He leaned forward and rested his elbows on his knees. "My dad just waylaid me on my porch."

"Oh, no."

"I told him I wasn't going to marry Rebecca."

"What did he say?"

He took a deep breath. "I have a week to get my stuff off of his property."

"Skyler! No. Oh my gosh. I'm coming over there right now."

He straightened up. "No. That's not a good idea."

"Then come here. Or meet me somewhere."

He thought for a moment. He didn't want her to go out this late at night. But he really needed to see her. "I can meet you at the rodeo grounds."

"Okay. In the stands by the main arena."

"But I need to go talk to Rebecca first. I'll text you when I'm leaving the ranch."

"Okay."

"I'll see you soon."

He got into the car and left his house and drove to the main house. He was afraid his father would be outside, but he wasn't, the house was dark. He went inside and up the stairs to Rebecca's door and knocked.

She opened it looking like she'd been sleeping. "Skyler? What are you doing here?"

"Let me in for a minute."

She looked like she was going to say no, which would've left him with the decision of whether to insist or not. But then she opened the door wider and took a step back.

Skyler went into the room. "I think you know why I'm here."

She pulled her robe closed across her chest and nodded. "Just get it over with, Skyler."

He sighed. "I can't marry you, Rebecca. I don't love you. And you don't love me. I don't know why I even let it get this far."

He expected some tears. But what he got was an eerie calm. "Is that all?"

"Um...yeah. That's it, I guess."

She returned to the door and opened it. "Then get out of my room."

"Okay." He stepped through the door. "You know I'm right. This whole thing was a setup from the beginning."

Rebecca closed the door without responding. Skyler stood there a moment, then headed down the stairs. His father was standing in the living room.

Skyler stopped walking. "I know. I'm going."

Leo didn't say anything and Skyler left the house and got into his car. He texted Abby, before leaving the property and driving toward the rodeo grounds. He was closer than Abby was. He'd get there before her.

Abby got dressed while she waited for Skyler's text. When it came, she slipped quietly out her door and down the hall to the stairway. She went down the stairs to the living room, then stopped when she saw a light on in the kitchen.

While she was debating on whether to sneak out or see who was in the kitchen, Deacon came out and spotted her.

"Abby?"

"Hi."

He took in the fact she was dressed and was wearing a jacket. "Kind of late to be going out."

She sighed and crossed the room to him. "It wasn't planned." She might as well come clean. "Skyler called me."

"Is he okay?"

"No. His stupid father just disowned him."

"What the hell for?"

"Because he's calling off the wedding, which will ruin Leo's business deal with the Greenwoods."

"Well, shit. It was probably a gut reaction. Leo's an ass. But that's beyond being an asshole."

"Well, he threatened it the other day. I'm not sure what went down tonight. But whatever it was, it happened fast."

"So, where are you going?"

"I'm going to see him. He's upset. As you can imagine."

"Right. Well, you know he's got a home here if he needs it."

Abby hugged him. "Thank you. And I'll tell him that. But he says his house is in his name. His grandfather left it to him."

"Okay. Where are you meeting him?"

"At the rodeo grounds."

Deacon kissed her on the forehead. "Just drive safe. "

"I will. I'll see you in the morning."

She went out the front door and got into her SUV. Everything would be alright. It had to be.

Twenty minutes later, she pulled into the rodeo grounds and drove to the main arena. She spotted Skyler's car and parked next to it. He came out of the shadows of the bleachers and met her at the car.

She hugged him. "I'm so sorry."

He stepped back from her and nodded. "It's a shock. You know? For him to actually do it."

She took his hand. "Let's go sit down."

"I'd rather walk."

"Okay." They started walking, and she glanced at him. "So, what happened? You must've barely gotten home."

"He was waiting for me on my porch. He knew where I'd been. I don't understand why he has such a problem with your family."

"Deacon says it goes way back."

"That's what my dad said."

"So, how'd you get from that to him kicking you out of the family?"

"I told him I wasn't going to marry Rebecca."

Abby was glad Skyler actually told him and didn't delay it. But now, she felt pretty responsible for the result. "Are you absolutely, one hundred percent sure?"

He stopped and took her hands. "Abby. I love you. I'm going to be fine. It's just the fact he actually followed through with his threat that's got me all...whatever. I don't know what I am."

She looked at him. "You love me?"

"Of course I love you."

She put her arms around his neck and kissed him, then laid her head on his shoulder. "I didn't know. I mean, I hoped. But I didn't know for sure."

"I've loved you since...I don't know. I think it was seeing you riding around the arena with your three rodeo queen sashes, giving the metaphorical finger to those other women. I couldn't help myself."

Abby laughed. "Oh my gosh." She moved back a foot. "I love you, too. I was just too stupid to realize it."

He kissed her more passionately than they had on the meadow. More passionately than she'd ever been kissed. She tried to breathe as the fireworks soared around her, then she backed away from him.

"We need to take a minute."

"Abby. I don't care about my dad or the Fremont Ranch. I care about you. I want to be with you."

"Okay. Me too." She hugged him again. "Me too. Did you talk to Rebecca?"

"Yes. It was weird. She was... She didn't react at all. Or try to talk me out of it."

"That is weird. But I'm glad she didn't make a scene."

"Yeah. That's what bothers me. I expected a lot more resistance. Tears. Begging." He smiled at Abby. "Not that I'm such a great catch. Just because it ruins her plans to be part of the Fremont family."

"Maybe she knew you meant it."

"Nah. I just hope she leaves tomorrow."

"And your dad?"

"He's probably at home right now, thinking I'll show up in the morning and beg him to reconsider."

"I want you to know, Deacon said our home is yours. Whatever you need. I know you have your house. But if you need to get away from the property for a few days. Or if you need to put the horses somewhere."

"That's very kind of him. How does he know what happened?"

"He caught me leaving the house. I had to tell him. I'm sorry. Maybe I shouldn't have."

"No. It's fine. I could probably use his advice on a few things."

"Whatever you need."

He took a deep breath. "Okay. Seeing you has made it easier. I don't feel so gut punched anymore."

"We'll figure this all out. Together."

"I like the sound of that."

They talked for a while longer, but it was late and Skyler didn't want to keep her out.

He kissed her. "You should go home."

She nodded. "I don't want to go. But you're right."

He walked her to the car. "Everything's going to be alright."

"I know." She smiled. "I love you."

He grinned. "I love hearing you say that."

He opened the door, and she got in behind the wheel. "Call me tomorrow."

"I will."

He closed her door, and she started the engine, then with a wave, she drove away. He loved her. And she loved him. How did she not realize it until now? "Everything is going to be alright."

Skyler was happy and at peace. Screw his father. He didn't need him or his money. He had Abby, and that's all he'd ever need. For the first time in a long time, he felt like he was in charge of his own destiny. Feeling at peace with the night's events, he went home and went to bed.

The sound of someone knocking on his door, woke Skyler. He put on his pants, then wandered out to the living room, and listened at the door. Whoever it was, knocked again.

"Who is it?"

"It's Russell, sir." Russell was one of the hands. He helped Skyler take care of his horses.

Skyler opened the door. "Is everything okay?"

Russell had his hat in his hands. "It's the horses, sir."

"What about them?"

"They're gone."

Skyler stepped out onto the porch. "What do you mean, they're gone?"

"I went to feed them this morning and the barn's empty. The stalls doors were all open. I swear, sir, I didn't leave them open. I'd never."

Skyler put a hand on Russell's shoulder. "I know it wasn't you."

"Then who, sir? Who would do such a thing?"

"I'll take care of it, Russell."

"Should I go look for them?"

"No. I'll go. Go back to work before you get in trouble with the old man."

Russell left the porch and got into his pickup, while Skyler sunk into one of the chairs. Someone let all of his horses go. There was only one person it could be. As stubborn and unforgiving as his father was, he'd never let something as valuable as Skyler's horses loose. He got to his feet, then went inside and got dressed. It was early. But he needed some help.

He got into his truck and left the house, then headed for the Starlight Ranch.

Chapter Seventeen

"You'd trust me with your car?"

When Abby heard a noise at her window, she assumed it was Patches. The screen had been replaced, but he'd probably returned to see if he could get in again. She rolled over and snuggled into her quilt.

"Go away, Patches."

When she heard the noise again, she sat up. It didn't sound like a cat scratching. It sounded like someone was throwing something against the glass. She went to the window and looked down at the yard, then opened her window.

"Skyler?"

"Hey. Sorry. I didn't want to knock on the front door this early."

"Why are you here?"

"I need your help. Rebecca let all of my horses go last night."

Abby leaned on the window sill. "She did what?"

"They're all gone. The stalls were all left open. I need to borrow a horse. And I was hoping you might come with me."

"Of course. I'll be right down."

Abby got dressed, then jogged down the stairs and went to the kitchen. Ruthie was there preparing breakfast.

"What's young Mr. Fremont doing standing in the yard like a lost puppy?"

"He's not a lost puppy. His ex-fiancé let all of his very expensive horses go last night. I'm going to help him round them up."

"Not without breakfast, Miss Abigale."

"There's not time."

"Go get your horses loaded. I'll bring it to you. You can take it with you. I'll pack you a lunch, too."

Abby kissed Ruthie on the cheek. "Thank you." She went out the back door and met Skyler in the yard, then they headed for the barn. "We can take the small horse trailer. Let's load up Aladdin and Nutmeg.

While Skyler hitched the trailer to his truck, Abby went to gather the tack they'd need. She put it in the back of the truck, then she and Skyler returned to the barn. As they were bringing the two horses out, Deacon came from the house.

"Ruthie told me what happened. What can I do to help?"

Skyler gave him a nod. "Abby and I are going to go look for them. I don't expect they got too far."

"Do you need another rider? I'm happy to help."

"No. Thanks. If we don't find them today, I might take you up on the offer."

"Okay. Good luck." He looked at Abby. "Keep your phone on you and stay in touch."

She patted her pocket. "I've got it."

He helped Skyler load the two horses while Abby went to fetch the food from Ruthie.

"I guess Abby told you want happened last night."

Deacon nodded. "Your father is a hard man. But, this...I'm sure he'll come around."

Skyler shook his head. "I don't think so. But, I'm okay with it. It's kind of a relief, actually."

Deacon looked at him for a moment. "It's a lot of pressure being the only son of Leo Fremont."

"That's for damn sure."

Deacon closed the rear of the trailer. "And how does Abby fit into all of this?"

Skyler took a breath. It was time to come clean with Deacon, as well. "I love Abby. And she says she loves me." When Deacon didn't say anything, he went on. "I know you probably have a problem with that, but we're both adults. And I'm tired of playing by everyone else's rules."

Deacon held up a hand. "Relax, Skyler. I don't have a problem with it."

"You don't?"

"Of course not. The only reservation I ever had with her relationship with you was your damn father. He's had a bug up his ass about us Carmichaels for years. Keep him and his attitude away from Abby. That's all I ask."

Skyler nodded. "Of course."

Deacon held out his hand and Skyler shook it. "I wouldn't have made you an honorary uncle to Thea if I didn't think you deserved to be part of the family. I'm glad you finally got your head straight about the whole fiancé thing."

"I don't know what I was thinking."

"You weren't thinking. That's the problem."

Skyler saw Abby approaching from the house and went to take the food from her. Abby continued on to Deacon and gave him a hug.

"I wasn't sure if I should leave you two alone or not."

Deacon laughed. "It's all good, Abigale. Go round those horses up."

———— ❧❦❧ ————

Abby and Skyler drove the horses to the Fremont Ranch and parked the trailer in front of the barn. They left the truck and Abby followed Skyler into the barn. The stalls housing Skyler's seven horses were all empty with the stall gates open.

Skyler stood in the middle of the barn and looked at the empty stalls. Abby came to him and hugged him. "We'll get them back. They know this is home."

"I'm just worried about them getting hurt. Or running into a mountain lion."

"We'll find them today."

Skyler stepped away from her and walked to a wooden post between the stalls. Sitting on top of it was the engagement ring he'd given Rebecca. He picked it up and showed it to Abby.

"I guess she wanted to make sure I knew she did it."

He returned the ring to the post. "Let's go." He grabbed several lead lines, then left the barn.

They unloaded and saddled the two horses, then set out across the meadow behind the barn. There was no way of knowing which way the horses had gone or how far they'd gotten. So Skyler figured their best bet would be to follow the trail he usually took when he took them for rides. Now he wished he'd done it more often so the horses would have a better sense of how to get home.

They took it slowly, looking for any sign of seven horses passing through. Skyler knew the five polo ponies would probably stick together. But he wasn't sure about his two equestrian trained horses. They were used to working alone.

Skyler and Abby stopped when they came to a small creek.

Abby glanced at him. "We should probably eat some of this food Ruthie packed for us."

"Sure." He dismounted and let Nutmeg get a drink. "I don't suppose she sent along some coffee."

Abby smiled. "Of course she did." She pulled out a thermos and handed it to Skyler.

He poured some coffee in the lid, and drank it, then filled it again and handed it to Abby. She took a sip, before handing a breakfast sandwich to Skyler.

"Have I mentioned that I love your Ruthie?"

"Yes. You have. She's the best, for sure."

They sat in the grass and ate their breakfast and shared the coffee. When Skyler was finished, he looked at Abby.

"You haven't changed your mind, have you?"

"About you and me?"

"Yeah."

"I'm here, aren't I?" She leaned toward him and kissed him. " I love you and your old house, and your snobby trust fund."

"And my missing horses?"

"Especially your missing horses. I even love your fancy car."

"Well, if you're nice to me. I might let you drive it someday."

She kissed him again. "You'd trust me with your car?"

"I trust you with my life. Although, currently, the car is worth more than I am."

"Not true. You, my love, are priceless."

He pushed her down into the grass and kissed her. She smiled and put a hand on his chest. "We've got horses to find."

"Hmm. Yes, we do. But when they're safe in the barn, we'll revisit this moment."

She got to her feet and held out her hand. "The sooner we find them, the sooner we can get to that."

He took her hand, and she pulled him to his feet. He put his arms around her. "One more for the road." He kissed her, then smiled. "I waited a long time for this."

"Was it worth the wait?"

"Definitely."

They mounted their horses and continued their search. By mid-afternoon, they still hadn't spotted the missing horses and Abby could tell Skyler was getting worried and frustrated. He took a deer trail up the side of an embankment and stopped at the top of it. The rise in elevation gave them a good view of the area they'd ridden through.

Abby pulled up beside him. "What do you think? Where should we go next?"

He checked the time on his watch. "In order to get you home before dark, we need to head back to the ranch."

"And then come all the way out here tomorrow? It seems like we're just covering the same area."

"We can take a different route tomorrow." He thought for a moment. "Or..."

"Or what?"

"Never mind."

"Skyler?"

"My dad's hunting cabin."

"Your dad has a hunting cabin?"

"That's what he calls it. He doesn't hunt when he's there. He flies his rich buddies in once a year by chopper and they spend a week drinking and fishing."

"He brings them in by helicopter?"

"Yep. That's my dad."

"Where is it?"

Skyler took stock of where they were. "About five miles west. But if we commit to that, there's no going back to the ranch tonight."

Abby shrugged. "Is there food and water there?"

"Yes. It's stocked. One of the men rides out here a couple times a month to keep an eye on the place. Everything should be working. No electricity. But water, food, and shelter fit for rich wannabe outdoorsmen."

"Let's go to the cabin. Then we can start fresh tomorrow, already here."

Skyler laughed. "I keep thinking the horses have found their way home while we're out here looking for them."

Abby took out her phone. "We could call."

"No service out here."

She checked her phone. "You're right. Which means I'll be in trouble with Deacon when I see him."

"He'll try you and be able to tell the phone's not working."

"Right. But he'll assume the worst. I fell off a cliff. Or drowned in a raging river."

"We don't have either of those on the property."

"Doesn't matter. He'll still think it."

Skyler got Nutmeg moving. "Let's go."

They followed the bluff for about a mile, then dropped back down to the valley floor. When they got within a couple miles of the cabin,

Skyler stopped Nutmeg and pointed toward a stand of trees. "I saw something. Might have been a deer. But if it was, it was a damn big one."

He got down from Nutmeg and handed the reins to Abby. After getting a handful of oats and a lead line from his saddle bag, he walked toward the trees. "Hey, boy. You going to come out of there? I bet you're wondering where your nice warm stall is. I've got a treat for you."

The horse stepped out of the trees at the sound of Skyler's voice.

"There you go Willie. Good boy." The horse looked at Skyler for a moment, then started walking toward him. Skyler held out the oats and Willie came to get them. While he ate, Skyler attached the lead to the halter. Willie finished the oats and Skyler patted his neck, then looked him over. "I think he's okay. I don't see any damage."

Abby walked Aladdin over to them, leading Nutmeg. She smiled at Skyler. "One down."

Skyler looked around. "I thought he and his buddies would stick together."

"They might still be close."

Skyler mounted Nutmeg. "Okay. Let's keep going. Keep an eye out for the rest of them."

They made it to the cabin without seeing anymore horses. It was more of a small lodge, then a cabin and Abby was surprised to see it here in the middle of nowhere. They put the horses in the small shed and fed them with the alfalfa that was there.

Skyler took her hand as they headed for the cabin. "Okay. You ready to check this place out?"

"It's quite impressive."

"My dad doesn't do anything half-assed. He's got to keep one up on his friends."

"Right." They went onto the large porch, then Skyler opened the door.

The inside was as impressive as the outside. They stepped into a large living space with a rock fireplace covering one wall, a kitchen along another, and three doors leading into three bedrooms.

"Wow."

"Yeah. It's not much smaller than my house."

"Well, we'll be comfortable." She crossed the room to the kitchen area. "Let's see what there is to eat."

"While you do that, I'll bring in some firewood."

Abby watched him go out the door, then went to look through the cupboards. They were full of non-perishables and she could've made a pretty fancy meal. But she'd never learned to cook. And even though Ruthie offered to teach her, she never had the interest. Being the good little wife who had dinner ready for her man when he came in from working all day wasn't her vision of any future relationship she wanted to be in.

She looked at the cans of beef stew in her hands. "Yet, here you are making dinner while Skyler's out gathering firewood." She'd slipped into wife mode without even thinking about it.

Chapter Eighteen

"You just made your first mistake."

S kyler brought the firewood in and got a fire started before join-ing Abby in the kitchen. She poured the hot stew into two bowls and handed him one.

"Just so you know. This is the extent of my cooking skills."

He laughed. "You grew up with a cook preparing all your meals. That doesn't surprise me."

"Still, I'm twenty-two years old. I just never saw myself in the roll of Suzy Homemaker."

"I figured that out about you a long time ago."

She leaned against the counter and took a spoonful of stew, then blew on it before putting it in her mouth. After she swallowed, she glanced at Skyler.

"Did Rebecca cook for you?"

He laughed. "I'm pretty sure Rebecca doesn't know how to operate a can opener, let alone a stove." He set his bowl down and stepped close to Abby and put his hands on her arms. "I love you for who you are. I don't expect you to change into someone you're not to fit the norm of what society thinks you should be."

"And I never thought I would. But here we are in this cabin and the first thing I did was come make dinner for you while you went and got the wood. It's so...conventional."

He smiled, then kissed her on the forehead. "Next time. You can go get the firewood and I'll open the can of stew."

She smiled. "Okay. Deal."

They took their bowls and went to sit by the fireplace.

Abby glanced at Skyler. "I didn't mind it, though."

"Abby. We'll figure it out. And we'll do it without turning you into Suzy Homemaker."

She ate some more stew. "You grew up with a cook, too."

"Yes, I did. But I've learned how to feed myself since I came back from Harvard and moved into my house. It seemed a little pretentious to hire a cook just for me."

"Yeah. You're probably right."

"And now, of course, I can't afford to."

"So, assuming your father doesn't change his mind, what are you going to do?"

"I don't know. But I'll figure that out, too."

She studied him for a moment. "It seems you're handling this whole disinherited thing pretty well. But you have to be a little freaked out about it."

Skyler thought for a moment while he finished his stew and set his bowl aside. "I'm really not. I'm actually kind of excited. For the first time in my life, I get to make my own decisions. I may make some bad ones. I'll certainly make some mistakes. But hopefully I'll learn from them and find my own path."

Abby set her bowl down and went to him and sat in his lap. She put her arms around his neck and kissed him. "I hope I can help you with some of those decisions."

"I want you to help me with all of them."

She smiled. "Okay. But the mistakes are on you."

"I'll take full responsibility." He pulled her in close and kissed her, then grinned. "Now adios these dishes into the kitchen."

She shook her head and pointed at him. "You just made your first mistake."

They washed the dishes together, then went onto the porch and sat on the swing to watch the sun sink down behind the trees. The sky was a brilliant pink, and Abby sighed as she laid her head on Skyler's shoulder.

"This place is wasted on rich guys who will never appreciate how beautiful it is."

"I know. It's a shame. They come up here and drink and play cards. Talk business. Make deals. Men like my father never take the time to sit on the porch and watch the sun go down."

"So, with all this future planning we need to do. There's one thing we have to do."

"What's that?"

"Make time to watch the sun go down."

"It's pretty amazing coming up, too."

She shook her head. "That would require getting up with the rooster."

"Maybe just once in a while?"

"Okay. Once in a while is fine."

He got to his feet. "I'm going to check on the horses before it gets too dark."

Abby stood too. "I'll come with."

They held hands and walked to the horse shed to make sure the horses were secure. Then they headed back to the house and went inside. Skyler put another piece of wood on the fire and they sat together on the couch.

"I'm glad you're here with me, Abby."

"So am I. And we'll find your horses tomorrow, or we'll go back and they'll be in the barn."

"I need to move them before I'll be able to get my barn in shape. Do you suppose I can keep them at the Starlight?"

"Of course. Or better yet. You can put them at the O'Hare Ranch. Winston has sold a few horses and isn't buying anymore. He's got quite a few empty stalls."

"Cassidy's grandfather, right?"

"Yes. He's about to turn it over to her, and it will be assimilated into the Starlight."

Skyler laughed. "That should make my dad super jealous. He's about to be left in the dust. Especially if his deal falls through with Bruce Greenwood."

"Do you think it will?"

"I don't know. I hope so. But if it was all hinging on Rebecca and I getting married, then it wasn't much of a deal in the first place."

Abby put her hand on Skyler's leg. "Why do you suppose your father hates our family so much?"

"I don't know. He'd never tell me. And believe me, I've asked. My mom did allude to the fact once that he and your dad were friends when they were young. They went to high school together and did rodeo. I'm pretty sure he knew your mother, too."

"That's interesting. I think Deacon knows a little about it. But he's never chosen to share that information with me. He says he doesn't know. But I'm sure my dad talked to him about it."

"Hmm. We may never know the truth."

She laid her head on his shoulder. "I guess it's up to us to make sure the future generations of Carmichaels and Fremonts are joined together." She sat up and looked at him. "I didn't mean..."

He smiled and put a hand on her cheek. "I feel the same way, Abby. Ever since our walk after Tobias' wedding, I can't see a future without you in it."

She smiled and nodded. "But we'll take it slow, right?"

"Of course. I'll follow your lead."

"I realized two things recently. One is that I've spent more time with you than I have with any other man I wasn't related to. And two, that you're my best friend. And when something happens, you're the first person I want to call and talk to about it."

He stared at the fire for a minute. "So, when I didn't tell you right away about Rebecca, it really hurt your feelings."

"It did."

He looked at her. "I'm sorry. I won't ever keep anything from you again."

"That might be an impossible promise to keep. But thank you for making it. Just don't keep the big stuff from me."

"Okay. You got it."

It was getting late, and they'd spent a long day in the saddle. When Abby yawned, Skyler smiled at her.

"I think you need to go to bed."

"It's so nice sitting here with you. I don't want it to end."

"It's the first of many evenings we'll spend sitting in front of a fire."

She sighed. "Alright." They both stood and Skyler took her hand. "I'll let you have my dad's room. It's the nicest."

"Actually. That's kind of creepy. I'll take one of the others."

He laughed. "Okay. You're right. I don't want to sleep in there either."

"Take the one on the right. It has a bathroom. I'll be right next door."

"In case I see a monster under my bed?"

"Yeah. In case of monsters." He kissed her and handed her a candle. "Sleep well, Abby."

"You too." She squeezed his hand, then went into the bedroom and closed the door. She sat on the bed and wondered how many old men had slept in it. "Okay. Don't think about it. I'm sure the bedding's been changed."

She hadn't planned on being out all night, so she had nothing but her clothes she was wearing. She took off her boots and her jeans, then carried the candle into the bathroom. It had a gravity flush toilet and a sink with a hand pump to bring water to the sink. She washed her hands and rinsed her face and called it good. There wasn't much else she could do.

She got into bed and snuggled into the layers of blankets and quilts. The bed was comfortable, and she'd probably sleep pretty well. She closed her eyes, then opened them again. She wasn't tired, and she was no longer thinking about who else had slept in the bed. She was thinking about Skyler. They'd professed their love for one another and they'd pretty much agreed what they had was going to last forever. Even though it'd only been a few days since their relationship had changed, she wanted to be with him. She needed to be with him, and she didn't want to wait any longer.

She got out of bed and picked up a blanket from the end of it. After wrapping it around her shoulders, she picked up the candle and opened the bedroom door. The house was dark. Skyler had gone to his room.

She took a breath to calm herself. She was scared, and excited, and anxious, and so ready to be with him. She went to his door and knocked softly.

A few moments later, he opened the door. "Abby?"

She looked up at him. "Can I stay with you?"

He gave her a small smile. "Don't tell me there are monsters under your bed."

"I don't know. I didn't look. I just know I don't want to be alone."

He opened the door and let her in, then took her hand and whispered, "Abby?"

She smiled. "I'm kind of winging it here. Can I just lie with you and..."

"Come on." He took the candle and blew it out, then got into bed. She laid down next to him and he put his arm around her as she laid her head on his chest. It felt so good and so right to be in his arms. She wasn't scared anymore, or even anxious.

"I'm a little..." She laughed. "I don't know what I am."

"Shh." He kissed her forehead. "Just relax. If all we do is sleep, I'm fine with that. I love that you're here. I love that you trust me to be here with you."

"Thank you. I do trust you. I always have." She was quiet for a few minutes. "Skyler?"

"Yes."

"I want you to be my first. And my only. And my last."

"I'm here, Abby. Now and forever."

Chapter Nineteen

"I think that's a family trait."

When Abby woke up, the sun was coming through the curtains. She didn't know how late it was, but she was pretty sure they'd slept in. She looked at Skyler, who was still asleep. Everything about him was so perfect. She'd always known he was a good-looking guy, but now, seeing him lying next to her with nothing but a blanket on, she was overwhelmed by the sheer beauty of his body. How could anyone be this flawless? She reached for him and ran a hand down his arm.

He opened his eyes. "Hey."

"I didn't mean to wake you."

"It's okay." He rolled over and stretched, then looked at the window. "Judging by the sun, I think it's mid-morning."

"Well, we were up pretty late last night." She smiled. "You know the song that says something about your body being a wonderland?"

"Yeah."

"I get it now." She put a hand on his chest. "I want to get to know every inch of you."

He raised up on an elbow. "I'd be okay with that. But of course fair is fair, so..."

Abby giggled. "I'm still a little shy."

He laughed. "After last night?"

"Yes. This is all new to me. I'm not used to parading around in front of someone."

"First off. I'm not someone. And secondly, you don't need to parade. I'd be happy with a glimpse or two."

"Can we work our way up to that?"

"Sure. We'll do some tentative exploring later, when you're done being shy." He kissed her, then got out of bed. When she squealed and put a hand over her eyes, he laughed. "Abby. You're so cute."

She peeked through her fingers, then dropped her hand. "Okay. Alright. Not bad."

"Not bad?"

She smiled. "Pretty damn impressive, actually."

He grinned. "Thank you."

She held a blanket to her chest. "Get dressed or we'll never get on the trail."

He sighed, then put on his clothes while she watched him. As he slipped on his boots, he said, "I'm going to start some coffee, then I'll go check the horses. You get dressed without me looking on."

"Thank you."

"But don't make a habit of it."

"I won't."

Skyler left the room and went to the kitchen to light the gas stove. He filled the percolator with water and coffee, then set it on the burner. Before he went to the front door, he glanced toward the bedroom. Last night was better than he could've ever imagined. And it was just the beginning. Abby was finally his.

He opened the front door and lost his smile when he saw Deacon and Tanner standing on the porch.

"Oh, shit." He put a hand to his chest. "You scared the bejesus out of me."

Deacon laughed. "Sorry. I was just about to knock."

"What are you doing here? And how'd you know we'd be here?"

"Well, when Abby didn't come home last night, I figured you stayed out. And the only reason you'd do that is if you hadn't found the horses. So, we came to help."

"But how'd you know about the cabin?"

"I've heard about it. Your dad's not too shy when it comes to bragging about his many assets."

"Right."

"But, regardless of all that. Looks like you didn't need our help after all."

Skyler stepped out and closed the door behind him. "What do you mean?"

Deacon nodded toward the horse shed. The six missing horses were standing there next to Willie, Nutmeg, and Aladdin.

"Damn. They must've come in last night. When we went to bed, I only had one of them."

Deacon looked at Skyler. "Is Abby up?"

"Um...I think so."

The door opened and Abby came out fully dressed with two cups of coffee in her hands. "Hey, guys. What are you doing here?"

Deacon studied her for a moment. "I was worried when you didn't come home. We set out this morning at daybreak."

"I would've called but, no service."

Deacon seemed to be trying to discern if all was as it seemed. "Yeah. I figured. Still, we wanted to make sure you were okay."

She smiled. "I'm fine, Deacon. Do you want to come inside and have some coffee?"

He glanced at Skyler. "Sure."

Deacon followed Skyler inside, and Abby glanced at Tanner, who was grinning.

Abby scowled at him and whispered, "What?"

"Nothing."

"Tanner."

"Don't worry. Deacon has his 'what I don't know won't hurt me blinders' on." He lowered his voice. "But I know exactly what happened here last night."

Abby punched him in the shoulder. "Shush."

He grinned as he rubbed his arm. "The man's only been single for twenty-four hours."

She swung at him again, but he dodged out of the way, then went into the house. She followed him in and closed the door a little harder than she needed to. Skyler had poured two more cups of coffee and he handed them to Deacon and Tanner.

"Thank you for coming out here. It'll be nice having help to get them back to the ranch."

Deacon nodded. "Not a problem." He looked around the cabin. "This place is nice. It's bigger than I thought it'd be."

"My dad doesn't do small. Bigger is better. That's his motto."

Abby set her cup down. "Skyler needs somewhere to keep the horses until he gets his barn fixed up. I thought maybe he could keep them at Winston's. He's got room, right?"

"For seven horses. Sure. That should be fine. It's closer to your house, too."

"Yeah. I need a couple of weeks to get my barn in shape. Dad gave me a week to get them out of his barn. But I'd just as soon move them now. Can we take them right to Winston's barn?"

"I'll call him as soon as we have phone service. I anticipated you might want to move them out of your father's property and we brought the big horse trailer with us this morning. With that and the small trailer you brought Nutmeg and Aladdin over in, we'll be able to move them all."

"Thank you."

"So, you left the trailer at Dad's barn?"

"Yep. He came out of the house when we pulled in. Ready to give me hell. But when I explained to him you two had been out all night, he really couldn't deny me access to his land. And even if he had, it wouldn't have stopped us."

Tanner laughed. "It was a little tense for a minute or two. I was half expecting Deacon and your old man to come to blows."

Skyler grinned. "I would've love to have seen that."

Deacon nodded. "I wouldn't have minded too much myself. But it's probably better it didn't come to that."

"I guess."

Deacon drained his cup. "We should probably get a move on."

Abby gathered the cups. "Tanner, help me get these cups washed while Deacon and Skyler go get the horses ready."

He sighed. "You can't wash four cups."

"Just help me."

He nodded. "Sure. Fine."

Deacon and Skyler left, and Abby looked at Tanner. "Please don't say anything to anybody."

"Of course. I'd never. Don't worry about it."

"Thank you."

"So, are you guys officially together, then?"

"Well, duh."

He laughed. "I'm happy for you."

She smiled. "I'm happy for me, too."

"I've always liked Skyler. And God knows, he's been patiently waiting for you for a year and a half."

"I really, really like him."

"Are you in love with him?"

She nodded. "Yeah."

"Cool."

She hugged him. "Thank you for being my cool and sweet little brother."

"You're welcome. But if the time ever comes, where I need you to be discreet...?"

"I've got your back, Tanner. Always."

They headed for the door. "Are we really going to have a Harvard man in the family?"

"A Harvard man and a Fremont. Tobias is going to have a stroke."

As they were getting the horses saddled, Deacon glanced at Skyler. "I'm not going to ask what happened here last night. But I want to make sure you know how much Abby means to me and her brothers. And that we'd do most anything to keep her safe."

Skyler looked at him. "So would I."

Deacon nodded. "See that you do."

Abby and Tanner came up to them and Deacon handed her Aladdin's reins. "He's all ready for you."

"Thank you." She glanced at Skyler and he gave her a wink. "Let's get these horses to their new home. Or their new temporary home."

They all mounted their horses and headed out with the seven horses staying close. They seemed to sense they were safe and headed home. Deacon and Tanner took the lead and Skyler and Abby rode behind, keeping the other horses in a close group between them.

Abby looked at Skyler. "So, do you think Deacon knows?"

Skyler nodded. "He knows."

She sighed. "And you're still alive. I guess that's a good sign."

He laughed. "I was a bit nervous for a minute or two."

"Deacon can be intimidating. But he's a romantic at heart."

"I think that's a family trait."

She laughed. "We'll add it to our crest. Family, loyalty, and romance."

"That sounds about right."

It took a couple of hours to get to the ranch and as they approached, Skyler was hoping his father wouldn't be there waiting for them. They arrived at the trailers and while Deacon, Tanner, and Abby loaded the horses, Skyler went into the barn to gather their tack. He couldn't take it all on this trip. But he wanted to get started on moving it out of his father's barn. When he heard someone behind him, he turned to find his mother.

He set down the saddle he was holding and gave her a nod. "Mom."

"Skyler. Your father told me what he did."

"You mean kick me out?"

"He said he gave you a choice."

"Right. He did. Marry Rebecca so his deal goes through with Bruce Greenwood, or leave."

"He was upset. He didn't mean it."

Skyler shook his head. "Of course he meant it. If he didn't, he'd be here right now asking me to stay."

"Would you stay? If he asked you to?"

He took a moment to answer her. Despite her being there talking to him, he knew she believed he should do what his father wanted and marry Rebecca. "No. I'm done. I'm done with Dad trying to manipulate me into being someone I'm not. He put a business deal over my happiness. He basically used me as a bartering chip. So, no. I don't want any part of him or this ranch. And if you choose to back him on this, then I guess I'm done with you, too."

"Honey." She went to him and put her arms around him. "We only want what's best for you."

He took a step back. "I don't believe that. What's best for me is standing out there by the horse trailer. If you can't understand that. Or give me your support. Then I don't think there's anything else to say."

She nodded. "If you leave. There will be no coming back."

"I know. I'm fine with that. You've obviously made your choice to stand with Dad."

"He's my husband."

"And I'm your son."

She turned and walked away from him. Skyler took a deep breath, then picked up the nearest thing he could find, which was an aluminum bucket, and tossed it across the barn.

Abby came up behind him and put her arms around him. "I'm so sorry."

He turned and hugged her. "God help me if I ever treat our kids like this."

She pulled back and looked at him. "Kids?"

He gave her a smile. "I figure three or four. What do you think?"

"I think I love you."

Chapter Twenty

"How long was I gone?"

Abby and Tobias were walking down the sidewalk. He and Gemma had gotten back two days ago and Abby brought him into town to buy him lunch. She figured she'd fill him up with some good food before telling him about her and Skyler. She'd asked Deacon and Tanner to let her be the one to tell him.

Tobias glanced at her. "You say you missed me. But I was only gone a few days. So why are you really buying me lunch?"

"Can't a girl buy her brother lunch?"

"What's up, sis?"

She stopped walking. "Well, I was going to wait until we'd eaten, but—" She stopped when she saw Leo headed for them. It didn't look like a random meeting. He was walking right for them and he didn't look happy. "Oh, shit."

Tobias turned to see what she was looking at. "What the hell does he want?"

Leo strode up and stopped two feet in front of Abby. "I hope you're happy, Miss Carmichael."

Tobias took a step toward him. "Back up Leo. What's this about?"

"It's about your sister taking advantage of my son and messing with his head so he doesn't know what's what." Leo hadn't moved back, and Tobias put a hand on his chest.

"Back the hell up."

Leo scowled, then took a step back. "Like a true Carmichael. She takes what she wants and doesn't care about the chaos she leaves in her wake."

Tobias smiled at him. "Seems to me that describes the Fremonts, not the Carmichaels. I've been gone for a few days, and apparently I missed some things. But if this has to do with Skyler walking away from the marriage you arranged for him in order to be with my sister, then I'd say the man is old enough to make that decision for himself."

"My son has a responsibility to his family. He has obligations that don't include messing around with a Carmichael."

"Messing around?"

"Yes. Your sister is—"

Tobias punched Leo in the nose, and the man dropped onto the sidewalk with a groan.

Abby took Tobias' arm. "Oh my God." She looked down at Leo who was still sorting through what just happened.

Tobias shook his hand. "Damn hardheaded bastard."

Leo's head seemed to clear and he put a hand to his nose, which had started to bleed. Then he looked up at them, and got to his feet. He took a handkerchief from his pocket and held it to his nose. "If Skyler thinks you can offer him something better, then you're welcome to him. If he chooses you over his own family, then he's no son of mine."

Leo walked away and Tobias looked at Abby. "So, you gonna tell me what the hell is going on?"

She kept hold of his arm and led him across the street to the café. They went inside and took a table near the back. When the waitress came to offer them coffee, they both nodded.

Tobias checked his hand, which was beginning to swell around the knuckle of his middle finger which was slightly out of place. "I don't suppose you have a bag of ice?"

She smiled. "Coming right up." She leaned in close to him. "I'm glad somebody finally put that man in his place."

Tobias looked at her. "You saw that?"

She glanced at the window. "I had a front-row seat. Along with everyone else in the restaurant. There may have been some cheering as Mr. Fremont hit the ground."

Tobias looked around and seemed to take stock of who was there. He got a few nods and a couple hat tips. "Looks like mostly friendly faces."

"Most everyone in town would take a Carmichael over a Fremont if it came down to a vote."

Tobias grinned. "Good to know." She left to get their coffee and the ice for his hand and he smiled at Abby. "So, am I to assume you and Skyler have come to an agreement?"

"Yes. Skyler and I are...together."

He raised an eyebrow. "How long was I gone?"

"Let me give you the condensed version. We kind of figured it out the night of your wedding. Then he went home and broke up with Rebecca and got disowned by Leo. Although, it wasn't in that order. Leo found out what Skyler was going to do and disowned him before he had a chance to talk to Rebecca."

"Okay. Sounds like typical Leo."

"Then Rebecca let all of Skyler's horses go in the middle of the night, so we went out the next day to find them."

"Jesus! Did you get them back?"

"Yes. They're now safe in Winston's barn and Rebecca has gone back to Dallas."

The waitress returned with their coffee and a small bag with crushed ice in it.

Tobias smiled at her. "Thank you."

Abby watched him put the ice on his knuckles. "I can't believe you punched him."

He shrugged. "The man's had it coming for a while." He took a sip of his coffee. "So what does this mean, exactly? You and Skyler."

"We're in love."

He nodded. "Okay."

"You don't have a problem with that?"

"Nope. Not at all. Did you think I would?"

"Well, you aren't always nice to him."

Tobias grinned. "It's all in fun. The man can't help what family he comes from. And I suppose I can overlook the whole Harvard thing."

Abby shook her head. "How gracious of you."

"Anything for you, sis."

They ordered some lunch and were halfway through it when the local deputy sheriff came into the restaurant and headed for their table. Tobias had gone to school with Mitch, and they were still friends. But the chief deputy was friends with Leo. So when Mitch approached them, Abby knew exactly why he was there. Leo had filed a complaint with his buddy, the chief.

Tobias gave Mitch a nod. "Mitch. How's it going?"

Mitch took off his hat and glanced at Abby before looking at Tobias. "I'm sorry, man."

"For what?"

"I've got orders to bring you in to the station."

Tobias smiled. "You can't be serious."

"Sorry. Mr. Fremont filed a complaint."

"And what did he say happened?"

"He says you assaulted him."

Tobias shook his head and looked at Abby. "It was hardly an assault. I punched him. Because he deserved to be punched. He was coming after Abby. You would've done the same thing in my place."

"I'm sure I would've. But I still need to follow orders. You'll get your day in court to explain what happened. For now, I have to bring you in."

Tobias got to his feet. "Fine. Let's go."

"I don't want to have to cuff you."

"I'm not going to run, Mitch. I'm not an idiot."

"Right."

Abby stood, too. "Tobias?"

He smiled at her. "It's okay. Call Deacon."

She nodded and watched Tobias leave with Mitch. Then she sat down and called Deacon.

"Abby?'

"Yeah. Tobias needs you."

The sheriff's department was on the first floor of the court house building, which was a half-story above street level. There was a set of cement steps leading up to the double glass doors, and as Abby and Deacon started up them, Tobias came through the doors.

He smiled at them and jogged down the steps to meet them. "I guess I didn't need you after all."

"What the hell were you thinking?"

"He was in Abby's face. He wouldn't back up. He was insulting her. And our family."

Deacon nodded. "How'd it go in there?"

"Well, Chief Decker was trying to play hardball. But when ten people came in to tell him they were witnesses to what went down, he backed off."

"So, it's done?"

"No, he charged me with assault. I still need to go to court." He shrugged. "Totally worth the trouble."

"Well, I'd reprimand you for not using restraint. But I can't say I wouldn't have done the same thing."

They headed down the street, and Tobias patted Deacon's shoulder. "So, are we adopting Skyler? Or what?"

Deacon glanced at Abby. "Seems one way or another he's destined to become part of the family."

As they passed the café, the waitress came out with the rest of their meal boxed up for them.

"I thought you might still be hungry."

Abby took the food from her as Tobias reached for his wallet.

The waitress put a hand on his arm. "Duke Miller paid for it."

Tobias took out a twenty and handed it to her. "Then this is for you. Thank you."

"Anytime."

As they continued down the street, Deacon glanced back at her. "Did she not get the memo that you're a married man?"

Tobias grinned. "What can I say? When you got it, you got it."

Abby laughed. "Okay, on that note. Deacon, can you take the outlaw home please? I need to go see Skyler and tell him what happened."

"Sure."

"I'll be home in a while. Or I'll call if I'm going to be late."

As Deacon pulled out of town, Tobias looked at him. "So, how serious is this thing with Skyler?"

"I'm pretty damn sure he'll be our brother-in-law before the summer's over."

"Shit. That's fast."

Deacon stopped at the traffic light. "I don't think either you or I have a right to judge how fast a relationship can move."

Tobias laughed. "I guess you're right." He was quiet a moment, then asked the question that had been on his mind since he found out Gemma was pregnant. "How the hell are you not scared to death over this whole parenting thing?"

"Who says I'm not?"

"It's scary as hell, right?"

Deacon nodded. "I thought I'd be semi-prepared since I had a hand in raising Abby and Tanner. And you, to a degree. Actually, apparently, I'm still raising you." He shook his head. "But with Thea, it's different. The responsibility of it all is kind of crushing."

"That doesn't really help, Deacon."

Deacon laughed. "Well, the crushing responsibility is balanced and often overcome by overwhelming love."

"Yeah. I get that. I know I didn't create Riley. But damn, I love that kid. And I'd protect him with my life."

Deacon put a hand on Tobias' shoulder. "You're going to be fine. And Riley is your son and a Carmichael. Doesn't matter who created him."

"So, you'll do it again? Give Thea a brother or sister?"

"Damn right."

"I imagine Mother and Dad would be pretty pleased to see the family home filled up with a bunch of little Carmichaels."

"I'm sure they would be." The light changed, and Deacon started driving. "Now, if we can just keep you out of jail, we can get on with that."

"Yeah. I really don't want to meet my kid through a glass divider."

"How'd it feel?"

"Punching Leo?"

"Yeah."

"It was...awesome."

"I'm sorry I missed it."

Tobias looked at his swollen knuckles. "He's got a damn hard head, though. I think I broke something."

Chapter Twenty-One

"We might have to break that habit."

Skyler sat on the steps of his porch and looked up at Abby. "Tobias did what?"

"He laid your father out. Right there on Main Street."

"Shit." Skyler grinned. "I'm sorry I missed it."

Abby sat next to him. "So, you're not mad at Tobias?"

"Of course not. He was standing up for you, right? I can only guess what my dad was saying to make Tobias want to punch him. God knows I've wanted to punch him many times over the years."

She took his arm and laid her head on his shoulder. "I was afraid that you'd…"

"Abby, any loyalty I had left for my father disappeared the night he told me to get my things off his property." He kissed the top of her head. "So, Tobias is okay with you and me?"

"Yes. He is. He said he will even consider letting the Harvard thing go."

Skyler grinned. "No. He'll never let that go. Which is fine. It's our thing, and it's cool we have a thing."

"Alright. You guys are weird. But I can accept it if you can." She looked at the house. "So, are you finally going to let me see the inside of your house?" She'd been wanting to see the house since the night at the hunting cabin.

He stood and pulled her up. "Yes. I think it's presentable now. I wanted it to be perfect before I showed it to you."

She hugged him. "I don't care how perfect it is."

"I know. But still. When Rebecca started calling it my cabin and inferred she could never live here, I kind of let it go, just to mess with her."

"Wow. That's not juvenile at all." She took his hand. "Can we make a pact?"

"Sure. What kind of pact?"

"That we never mention her name again."

He shook her hand. "Deal. She will now and forever be referred to as that woman."

"But hopefully, we won't refer to her at all."

"Even better." They went up the porch steps. "So, this is the porch."

"Thank you for clarifying that."

He laughed. "It wraps all the way around the house. So we can watch the sun go up or down whenever we want."

He opened the door and Abby followed him inside to the over-sized living room. "This is nice."

He looked around. "It's not the Carmichael house, but I like it."

Abby checked it out. It seemed the furniture was new, probably bought by Skyler when he moved in. It consisted of a blue plaid couch and two blue chairs. There was also a coffee table, which was an old steamer trunk, and two end tables, each with a lamp sitting on them. A new woodstove was installed in front of the original brick fireplace. The walls were freshly painted and he wood floors had been refinished.

Skyler walked over to the fireplace. "The woodstove is much more efficient than the fireplace."

Abby nodded. "I like woodstoves. They're a lot cleaner than an open fireplace."

He took her hand. "Let me show you the kitchen." He led her into the large kitchen with windows along one wall, making it bright and cheery. The cabinets had been refurbished and were painted a pale green. It went well with the light gray walls. "What do you think?"

"I love it. Did you pick out these colors?"

"No. I had some help."

"From her?"

"No. From Ellie at the hardware store."

There was a farm style table and a big hutch which had nothing on its shelves. Abby smiled at him. "I'm very impressed. I'm surprised your hutch doesn't have your grandmother's china on it."

"Not really a china, guy. I'm more of a paper plate guy. Or eat right out of the pot, guy."

"Hmm. We might have to break that habit."

He took her hands in his. "Can you see yourself living here?"

She let go of his hands and put her arms around his neck. "I would live anywhere with you. But, I honestly love it. It's wonderful."

He kissed her. "Let me show you the bedrooms."

He gave her a tour of the three smaller rooms. One was completely empty. One had a small bed and a stack of boxes in it. And the third looked like he was planning on making it an office. It had an old desk and chair, and two bookshelves with only a few books on them.

"Is this Mr. Fremont's office?"

"If I ever have a need for one, yes. Come on. I want to show you the master bedroom."

It was bigger than the others and had its own bathroom. It was sparsely furnished with just a Queen-sized bed and a dresser.

He nodded toward the bed. "Want to check out the bed?"

She smiled, then walked to the bed, sat down, and bounced a few times. "Very comfortable."

He sat next to her. "You think so?"

"Yes."

He moved closer to her. "Have you gotten past your shyness?"

"I believe I have."

"Good. Because I think we should give the bed a test run."

They hadn't been together again since the cabin. "You do, huh?"

"Yeah. What do you think?"

"I think that's a very good idea."

He laid back and pulled her down next to him. "Your brothers aren't going to come banging on the door, are they?"

Abby laughed. "I told them I might be late."

"Hmm. You might be very late."

Tobias flinched and pulled his hand away from Gemma. "Shit. That hurts."

"You dislocated your knuckle."

He rubbed his hand. "Can you fix it?"

"I'm not a doctor."

"Yeah, but I trust you more than I trust doctors."

She looked at him. "You don't trust Dr. Hart?"

"No. He's fine. Doctor's in general."

"I'll pop it back into place for you as soon as you tell me how it happened."

He stood and walked a few feet away. "Are you sure you want to know?"

Gemma nodded. "I'm very sure. I know injuries. And one like this happens when you hit something or someone."

Tobias shook his head. "Man, you're good."

"Who did you hit?"

He sat back down next to her on the bed. "Leo Fremont."

She turned to him. "What?"

"He totally deserved it."

She stood and moved to the chair in the corner of the room. "I want to hear everything."

"He was being an asshole to Abby. He came right up to us on the street and started berating her."

"So, you punched him?"

"Yeah. You would've too."

She leaned back in the chair. "Is he okay?"

"Well, I guess since I hit him hard enough to dislocate my knuckle, he could have a broken nose."

"Did it bleed?"

"Yeah. Quite a bit."

She smiled and shook her head. "I understand that you were protecting Abby, but my love..."

"I know. I'm a husband and a father. I can't be punching people in the street, no matter how much they deserve it."

"Are you going to be in trouble for it? Doesn't seem like something Leo Fremont would let go."

"I was booked and released. Charged with assault."

Gemma got to her feet. "That's ridiculous."

"I know." He held his uninjured hand out to her. "Leo and the chief are friends. But there were a lot of witnesses. The charges will get dropped. Or certainly reduced."

She went to him and took his hand. "And what if they're not?"

"Then we'll deal with it. But I'm not worried. And honestly, it was totally worth it, no matter what it cost me."

She sat next to him. "Is this the first time you've been arrested?"

"Um...no. I went through a phase in high school. Got into some trouble."

"What did you get arrested for?"

"Disorderly conduct and defacing public property. I got a year's probation and eight weeks of community service. Which actually worked out great. I worked as a groundskeeper at the equestrian center. And that's when I discovered horse jumping."

"What did you deface?"

"I wrote some inappropriate things on the side of city hall."

"Such as?"

He shook his head. "I'm not going to tell you."

"How about a hint?"

"It had something to do with the mayor's daughter. And it was actually true. I wasn't making it up."

She cocked her head. "Do you know this from first-hand experience?"

He grinned. "Would you be jealous if it was?"

"How old were you?"

"Sixteen."

She patted his knee. "Then, no."

"I never did anything with Lisa Weller. I wanted to, but she shut me down."

"Thus the graffiti?"

"It was a very vulnerable stage in my life."

She picked up the bag of ice he'd laid on the bed and put it on his hand. "You'd just lost your father."

"Yeah. And getting rejected was a really big deal."

She kissed him. "I'm sorry."

Tobias shrugged. "It's okay. I dodged a giant bullet. You've been in Johnson's with me."

"Yes. Of course."

"You know the woman who is usually at the front checkout?"

"Yes."

"That's Lisa Weller. Johnson now. She married Bill's son."

"Oh. Yeah. You dodge the bullet alright."

Tobias laughed. "I love that sometimes, you're just as shallow as I am."

She set the ice aside. "Let's get this fixed."

"Is it going to hurt?"

"Yes."

He scowled at her. "You could've lied to me."

"It'll be over in a second." She grasped his hand and popped his knuckle into place.

He let out a curse, and she put a hand over his mouth. "Shhh. You're going to wake up Riley."

He whispered another curse. "That really hurt."

"It'll feel better in a minute." She handed him the ice. "Keep this on it until we go to bed."

"Are you sorry you didn't become a doctor?"

She looked at him for a moment. "No. I like what I do. And I'm lucky to be able to do it here. If I was a doctor, I'd be out of luck until Dr. Hart retired."

"So you're happy here. No regrets?"

"Tobias Carmichael, how can you even ask me that?" She pushed him onto the bed. "Do I not show you enough how happy I am?"

"I think I need you to remind me."

She kissed him and started unbuttoning his shirt. "If you insist."

He held up his hand. "Be careful. I'm injured."

"I happen to be a physical therapist. I specialize in working with injuries."

"Hmm. I'll leave it in your hands, then."

Chapter Twenty-Two

"She'll just try to talk me out of it."

Skyler was on his way to feed the horses at the O'Hare ranch when a car came up fast behind him. As the vehicle got close, he recognized it as his father's. When Leo flashed his headlights, Skyler pulled over to the side of the road and stopped his car. Leo pulled in behind him and got out.

Skyler sighed, then got out as well. "What do you want, Dad?" Leo had two black eyes and his nose was taped. Skyler had heard that Tobias' punch had broken it.

"I need to talk to you."

"You could've called."

"Would you have answered a call from me?"

"Probably not."

Leo took a few steps closer. "I wanted to let you know I've rounded up several witnesses to your friend Tobias Carmichael assaulting me on the street the other day."

"He didn't assault you. He just shut you up. Have you sunk so low that you're bribing witnesses now?"

"Are you willing to let your friend go to jail?"

"He's not going to jail. He has a whole restaurant full of people who saw what happened."

"Are you willing to bet his freedom on that?"

Skyler shook his head. "Just tell me what you want, Dad."

"I want you to come to dinner tonight with your mother and me."

Skyler folded his arms across his chest. "And why would I want to do that?"

"Maybe we can work out a deal. Keep Tobias out of jail."

He shook his head. "What are you up to?"

"Come to dinner. And I'll tell you."

"I have to think about it."

"Fair enough. Dinner's at seven."

The family had eaten dinner at seven for as long as Skyler could remember. "I know, Dad."

Leo nodded, then walked away and got into his car. Skyler waited for him to make a U-turn and head down the road before getting into his car.

He sat for a moment. "What the hell is he up to?"

Skyler found Abby at the training pen watching Tanner with a young horse. He tried to sneak up on her, but she heard him and turned around.

She smiled at the sight of him. "Hey. I didn't think I'd see you until later."

"Can we take a walk?"

She lost her smile. "What's wrong?"

"Nothing. I just need to talk to you about something."

Abby glanced at Tanner. "I'll be back in a bit."

Tanner waved without taking his eye off the horse he was working with, as Abby jumped down from the fence she was sitting on.

Skyler took her hand. "Can we go to the pond?"

"Sure."

He took her hand, and they headed down the path.

Halfway there, she nudged him. "You're killing me. What's going on?"

He glanced at her. "I saw my dad this morning."

"How's he look?"

"Like he has a broken nose." He grinned at the thought. It was about time somebody put him in his place.

"What did he want?"

They reached the pond and sat at the picnic table. "He wants me to come to dinner tonight?"

She turned toward him. "You can't go."

"He wants to talk about his case against Tobias."

"His case? He doesn't have a case."

Skyler shrugged. "He says he does. He's got friends who will testify Tobias started it."

Abby scowled. "That's not true. His friends will lie for him?"

"I don't know if he actually has these witnesses or not. Or if he's just bullshitting."

"So call his bluff. Don't go."

He took a moment. "I think I need to."

"Skyler. No."

"Abby, if it will save Tobias from going to jail on trumped-up charges, then I have to at least hear what he has to say."

She shook her head. "I don't like it. Please don't go."

He stood and walked away from the table. "I don't want this to become a thing between us. But I need to go."

She got up and went to him. "It won't be a thing." She hugged him. "I don't ever want anything to become a thing."

"Well, that might be impossible. But in this instance. Just trust that I won't get sucked in by Leo Fremont."

"I do. I trust you."

He put his hands on her waist and looked at her. "So, we're okay?"

She nodded. "Yes. Just call me the second you leave there."

"I will. I promise."

They headed back for the training pen and Abby took his hand. "Can you stay a while?"

"I wish I could. I need to spend some more time with the horses. Dad stopped me on the way over to feed them. So, I threw them some hay, then came right here."

"Okay." She walked him to his car. "I miss you."

He pulled her in for a kiss. "I wish you'd stay the night with me one of these nights."

"Deacon and Tobias have been super supportive about all this, but I don't want to take advantage of that."

"Abby. You're a grown woman."

She patted his chest. "We'll figure it out."

"Yeah. I suppose we will." He kissed her. "I'll call you later."

Skyler got into his car and she watched until she couldn't see him anymore, then headed back to Tanner. He was coming out of the pen leading the horse.

He stopped when he saw Abby walking toward him. "Is everything okay?"

She shrugged. "I'm not sure. Skyler is having dinner with his parents tonight."

"Really? I thought he was done with them."

"So did I. His father is threatening to turn the Tobias incident into jail time."

"Well, shit."

"But he intimated Skyler could prevent it somehow."

"By doing something Leo wants?"

"Yeah."

"It'll be fine."

She put her hands on her hips. "How do you figure? Skyler doesn't have the best track record for standing up to his dad."

"He broke up with Rebecca and got disinherited. I'd say that's sticking up for himself."

"I guess. But what if he's sorry? What if he's having second thoughts? What if he doesn't think I'm worth losing everything for?"

"Abby. That's not even possible."

"I hope you're right."

"I am. Trust me. I may not currently be in love. But I know what it looks like. Skyler loves you and he's not going to let his father interfere with that."

"You will be you know. Someday you'll find your firework person."

"I suppose that's true. But I'm not in any hurry. I'll settle for being an uncle and a brother-in-law for now."

"And a brother."

"That, too. And a horse whisperer."

Abby smiled. "You are one in a million, Tanner."

"As are you."

Abby shoved him. "Okay. Enough of that. Are you done for the day?"

"Yes. Want to help me set up the rails? I feel like doing some jumping."

"You got it."

As they were setting up the rails, Tobias and Gemma arrived in his truck and parked by the barn. Gemma headed for the house and Riley and Tobias joined Abby and Tanner at the arena.

"Are you working with Pale Rider again?"

"Yeah. Want to watch?"

"Sure. I'll go saddle him up for you."

Abby smiled at Riley. "Want to come help set up the jumps?"

Riley nodded, then slipped through the fence and joined them. As they were finishing up, Tobias came out of the barn leading both Pale Rider and Esmeralda.

Abby and Tanner watched him approach.

Tanner went to the gate. "Do you want Abby to ride Esmeralda?"

"No. I'm going to."

Abby came up beside Tanner. "Tobias."

"I'm ready."

"Then ride Pale Rider."

"No. Esmeralda and I have a ride to finish."

Abby looked toward the house. "Shouldn't Gemma be watching this?"

"She'll just try to talk me out of it." He mounted Esmeralda. "Open the gate."

Tanner opened the gate to the arena and Tobias walked the horse through it. Then he started trotting her around the edge of the fence.

Abby went to Riley. "Go get your mom. Tell her she needs to come out here."

When Tobias saw Riley headed for the house, he looked at Abby. "Dammit, Abby."

"She should see this. She's been working toward this day, too."

He took the horse around the edge of the arena again, while Tanner and Abby stood by the fence and watched him. When Tobias prepared to take the first jump, Abby held her breath and Tanner put his arm around her. As Tobias took the first jump, Gemma and Riley came up behind them, and Gemma gasped.

Abby grabbed her hand and the four of them watched Tobias run the course, as though it hadn't been almost seven years since his last ride on Esmeralda. After the last jump, he rode to the fence and grinned down at them.

"And that's how it's done."

Gemma looked up at him. "Get down here, cowboy."

"Am I in trouble?"

"No. I want to give you a hug."

Tobias dismounted and went through the gate as Gemma ran to him and hugged him. "You crazy man."

"I'm sorry. I just knew I was ready."

"You looked fantastic."

"Like I knew what I was doing?"

She nodded and hugged him again. "How's your leg?"

He rubbed his thigh. "I think it's fine. I guess I'll know in a while if it's not."

"How did it feel to jump again?"

"It felt damn good."

Tanner came up and put a hand on his back. "And Tobias is back."

"Well, we'll see. I don't think I'll be competing anytime soon. But that was a good trial run." He looked at Abby. "Let me see you take Pale Rider around the course a few times."

She smiled. "Now I feel like such an amateur."

"I know you've been getting pointers from Skyler. You know what you're doing."

Abby mounted Pale Rider and ran through the course twice before coming back to the fence.

Tobias grinned at her. "Show off."

She pointed at him. "Gala weekend. You, me, Skyler, and Deacon. A family showdown."

"You're on. That gives me four months to get in shape."

"You better use it. Because I'm coming for you."

"Do you want to put some money on who takes first?"

Abby thought about it for a moment and then they both said, "Skyler," at the same time.

Abby laughed. "We'll bet on who takes second."

Chapter Twenty-Three

"Then all is right with the world."

Skyler got to his parent's house at six-forty-five. He didn't want to spend too much time sitting around before the meal was served. He stepped onto the porch and knocked on the door. He didn't feel like walking right in was an option any longer.

His mother opened the door. "Honey. You don't need to knock."

"I'm pretty sure I do. Your husband disowned me, Mom, remember?"

She motioned for him to come inside. "Come in. He's in his office."

She walked with him to Leo's office door. "Leo, Skyler's here."

Leo glanced toward the door. "Leave us be, Helen."

She nodded and left Skyler standing outside the door.

Leo frowned at him. "Don't hover there in the doorway. Come on in." Skyler stepped inside and Leo waved toward a chair. "Take a seat."

Skyler remained on his feet. "I'd rather stand."

"Suit yourself."

"Just tell me why I'm here, Dad."

"Alright. We'll get right to it. I have a proposition for you."

Skyler folded his arms across his chest. "What is it?"

"First off. I want you to know just how much trouble young Mr. Carmichael is in. I've got several well-known and respected citizens of Connelly, who will swear in court Tobias came at me unprovoked."

"What did you have to pay these respected citizens to say that?"

Leo smiled. "Let's just say they owed me a favor. I've always told you to keep track of who owes you what. You never know when you might need to collect."

Skyler took a few steps toward him. "So, let me get this straight. These friends of yours are willing to lie in court for you?"

"If it comes to that, yes. But hopefully it won't." He pointed at Skyler. "You can prevent all of this."

"How so?"

"By coming back to the family."

Skyler smiled at him. "I didn't leave the family, Dad. You kicked me out."

"All water under the bridge, son."

"What do I have to do to be welcomed back into the family and save Tobias from getting railroaded by your paid witnesses?"

"Go spend a year at Rolling Hills. Learn the horse trading business."

"And?"

"Take some time to rethink your relationship with Rebecca."

Skyler laughed. "Is that all?"

"At the end of the year, if you're still determined not to marry her. Then we'll consider that to be the end of it. I won't force you to marry her. That was never my intention."

"Anything else?"

"That's it. Next year, you come back here and we start to expand into the horse business. Of course, along with this, you'll stay clear of the Carmichaels. All of them. What do you say?"

Skyler moved to within a few feet of Leo. "I say, go to hell."

"Skyler. You won't get another chance."

Skyler studied Leo for a long moment. "Goodbye, Dad." He turned and headed for the door.

"Don't walk away from me, son."

Skyler kept going and continued through the house to the front door. Helen came up to him.

"Where are you going? Dinner is ready."

"I'm not staying for dinner, Mom."

"Honey."

"Bye, Mom." He opened the door and went outside. Once on the porch, he took a deep breath of fresh air, then continued to his truck. It was done. He was free. And he left on his terms, not his father's. It felt damn good.

He left the ranch and headed down the road. When he came to the turnoff to Tobias's property, he took it and drove the five miles to the house.

Tobias had heard him coming and was on the front porch. He came off of it when Skyler pulled up, parked, and got out of the truck.

"Skyler? What brings you out here this time of night?"

"Sorry to drop in on you, but it's kind of important."

"Come on in."

Skyler followed Tobias into the house, where Gemma greeted him with a smile.

"Hi, Skyler. Is everything okay?"

Skyler nodded. "Yeah. I think it is. I have something for you." He took a small tape recorder out of his pocket and handed it to Tobias. "When you get a chance, give that a listen. It's basically my dad confessing to bribing witnesses to testify against you."

"The hell you say."

"I don't know who needs to hear it, but it should be of interest to someone. And should definitely get your charges dropped."

Tobias shook Skyler's hand. "Thanks, man. How'd you get it?"

"He asked me over to dinner tonight to bribe me into coming back to the ranch. Using your assault charges as leverage."

"What did he want you to do?"

"The same old bullshit. But mostly, to steer clear of your family. All of you."

Tobias nodded. "Which includes Abby?"

"Yeah. Especially, Abby."

Tobias put a hand on Skyler's shoulder. "I think you've just been promoted from honorary uncle to brother."

Skyler smiled. "That sounds good to me."

"Shall we have a beer to celebrate?"

"Sounds good."

Tobias handed the tape recorded to Gemma. "We'll be on the deck."

He grabbed two beers on the way through the kitchen and they went onto the deck. They sat down and opened their beers.

Skyler held his up. "To freedom."

"Yours or mine?"

"Both."

They sat for a few minutes and enjoyed the cool night air. After a while, Tobias broke the silence. "Has Abby told you we're in the process of taking over the O'Hare ranch?"

"Yeah. She said Winston is ready to retire and turn things over to Cassidy and Deacon."

"Yeah. He's always concentrated on horses. Buying, selling, limited training. But we'd like to expand that to more training and less buying and selling."

"Sounds good. He's got the facilities for it. With a little work and adding a professional sized arena, you could do really well with that."

"That's what we figure. We also figured it would be a great place to put you."

"Me? Really?"

"You and Abby, along with Tanner's weird communications skills. You'd make a hell of a team."

"Shit. I'm flattered as hell."

"You need something to do, right? Now that you're on your own. And we can't have our sister hanging out with a disinherited and unemployed cowboy."

"Yeah. You wouldn't want that."

"What do you say? Will you think about it?"

"I don't need to think about it. I'm in. All the way."

"Deacon figures we can work out some sort of partnership."

Skyler laughed. "A Fremont Carmichael merger. Who'd of thought?"

"We'll get together this week with Deacon and sort things out."

"Man, I don't know how to thank you."

"No need. You've proven your loyalty to us. You're family."

Skyler grinned. "When I marry Abby, maybe I should take her name instead of the other way around." He suddenly realized what he said and looked at Tobias.

"What's this now?"

"Um... I don't know where that came from. I swear. We haven't talked about that. Wow! Sorry."

Tobias laughed. "Calm down. I've made my peace with the fact my sister is going to end up with a Harvard man."

"So, you'll be okay with it when we do talk about it."

"I'll be okay with it. So will Deacon and Tanner."

Skyler sighed deeply. "Then all is right with the world."

Skyler stayed for one more beer, then said his goodbyes to To-bias and Gemma. His next stop was the Starlight ranch, but it was late now, so he parked at the end of the driveway and walked to the house. He'd only had two beers, but he hadn't eaten in a while, so he was feeling them more than he normally would. The fresh cool air helped, though, and by the time he arrived underneath Abby's bedroom window, he was pretty clear-headed. There was a ladder leaning against the house next to her window, and he smiled.

"That's convenient." He didn't want to scare her, though, so he picked up a handful of gravel from the driveway and started tossing pebbles at the window. It took several before Abby's face appeared in the window.

Skyler waved at her and she opened the window.

"What are you doing? I've been waiting all night for you to call."

"I'm sorry. I have so much to tell you. I wanted to talk to you in person."

"Everyone's in bed."

"I'll come in the window."

"You can't climb the tree. You'll kill yourself."

"I don't need to climb the tree. There's a ladder." He went to the ladder and moved it under her window and started climbing it. When he got level with the window, he smiled at her through the screen. "Hey, there."

She smiled. "You'll need to take out the screen."

"No problem." He took a moment to wrestle the screen from the window, then dropped it to the ground. Abby opened the window more, and Skyler climbed through.

Abby hugged him. "Hi."

He kissed her. "Hi." He stepped away from her and looked around her room. "Wow. This is something. I had no idea your rooms upstairs were so big."

"Is that why you're here? To check out my room?"

He turned back to her. "No." He looked at her t-shirt and pajama pants. "Aren't you cute?"

"Well, if I'd known you were coming, I would've gone for something more appealing."

He shook his head. "No. This is very appealing." He took her in his arms again and kissed her.

After a moment, Abby pulled away. "You came here to tell me something."

"Yes." He took her hand, and they sat on the couch. "So, I went to my dad's house."

"Right. How'd that go?"

"I didn't stay for dinner. In fact, I only stayed about ten minutes."

She studied him for a moment. "It was that bad?"

"He offered to call off his witnesses if I go spend a year at the Greenwoods horse ranch."

"A year?"

"Yeah. And during that year, I would hopefully rekindle my relationship with Rebecca."

Abby shook her head. "Oh, is that all?"

"No. I also need to cut off all ties to the Carmichael family."

She smiled. "Yet, here you are."

"Yes. Here I am."

"So you told him—"

"To go to hell."

Abby hugged him.

He smiled at her when she pulled back, but didn't let her get to far away. "But wait, there's more. I had a tape recorder in my pocket and I recorded my father admitting to paying off his witnesses."

"Oh my God."

"Yeah. The reason I'm so late is that I took it right to Tobias."

She moved back away from him. "So you've been with him all night."

"Yeah. For the last couple of hours. Sorry. We had a couple of beers."

She cocked her head. "Only a couple?"

"I didn't eat dinner. So, yeah, only two on an empty stomach."

"You must be starving."

"A little bit, yeah."

She got to her feet. "I'll go get you something to eat."

He reached for her hand. "I don't want to get you in trouble with Deacon."

"He's in bed. It's fine."

Abby left Skyler in the room and went downstairs to the kitchen. She put together a sandwich, grabbed a bag of chips, and a bottle of soda. As she was leaving, Tanner came into the kitchen.

He looked at the food in her hands. "Hungry?"

"Um... Yeah. A little."

Tanner raised an eyebrow. "You know my bedroom is right next to yours, right?"

She hesitated before answering him. "Yeah."

"I heard you talking to Skyler outside your window."

"Please be cool about it."

He raised a hand. "I'm cool."

"He just wanted to tell me some stuff in person instead of on the phone."

"What stuff."

"He's still telling me."

"Okay. Fine. Go have a nice long *talk* with Skyler."

"Tanner?"

He shook his head. "I know nothing."

Abby returned to her room and while Skyler ate his sandwich, he told her what Tobias said about Winston O'Hare's ranch. Abby was excited, and they spent another hour talking about the possibilities of having a high end horse training facility would offer.

When they both started yawing, Skyler smiled at her. "I guess I should go. I'm kind of tired. It's been a long day."

"Yeah. For me, too."

He stood and gave her a kiss, then headed for the window. Abby followed him. But when he went to open it, she put a hand on his back.

"Skyler?" He turned to her. "Don't go."

He grinned. "Are you sure?"

"Yes. I want you to stay."

He closed the window. "All of a sudden, I'm not so tired."

She put her arms around his neck. "Good. Because I've got some exploring to do."

Chapter Twenty-Four

"It only took me fifteen years."

The plan was for Skyler to sneak out of the window before everyone got up. But when Abby opened her eyes, she knew they'd slept in past daybreak.

She patted him. "Skyler?"

He moaned as he reached for her. "Can't get enough of me, huh?"

"It's morning. The sun's up."

Skyler opened his eyes. "Oh shit."

Abby laughed. "New plan. Wait until we're all eating breakfast."

"What about your men? Someone is bound to see me."

"They're all out chasing cows. You should be fine. Just watch out for Ruthie. Go the long way around the house to avoid the kitchen."

"Okay. So how long until breakfast?"

Abby checked the time. "We have an hour."

"Hmm. I think I can work with that."

When it was time for Abby to go down to breakfast, she got dressed and kissed Skyler goodbye. She didn't want to kiss him goodbye. She wanted to stay there with him all day. But she had two brothers, a sister-in-law, and a nosy cook waiting for her downstairs.

"Be careful going down the ladder. I don't want you to get hurt."

He grinned. "That might slow us down a little."

Abby shook her head. "We'd figure out something."

He pointed a finger at her. "You're so bad. I love that about you." He raised up onto an elbow. "Do you want me to put the screen back in?"

"No. I'll have Hank do it. The thing falls out all the time. That's why the ladder is still there."

"Quite convenient. I must say. Last night was...great."

"I agree." She kissed him again. "Come back later. I'm working with Pale Rider after lunch."

"I'll be here."

She patted his chest. "I'm so excited about everything."

"Me too. We made it Abby. Despite me being an idiot for nine months. We made it."

She kissed him. "I'll see you later." They'd definitely made it, and she was happier than she ever imagined she could be.

Skyler got dressed before looking out the window to make sure the coast was clear. When he didn't see anyone, he backed out the window and started down the ladder.

About halfway down, he heard, "Let me hold this for you."

He looked down to see Deacon at the bottom of the ladder.

He stopped descending. "Shit."

Deacon motion at him. "Come on down nice and slow. I don't want to have to pick your ass up off the ground before I get a chance to kick it."

Skyler sighed, then continued down the ladder and as he got to the bottom, Deacon took a few steps back and folded his arms across his chest.

"Deacon, I—"

"Save it. Aren't you a little old to be sneaking out of windows?"

"I swear, I just came here to talk to her. To tell her what my dad said."

"You talked all night, did ya?"

"Um..."

Deacon relaxed his stance. "I talked to Tobias this morning. He told me what you did for him."

"Yeah. It's the least I could do."

Deacon glanced up at the window, then looked at Skyler for a long moment. "Next time, use the front door."

"Right. Of course."

Deacon turned and started walking away from him, then glanced back. "Are you coming? Ruthie will set another plate for you."

"Yeah. Right behind you."

He followed Deacon through the house and into the dining room. When Abby looked at him, he gave her a small shrug.

She sat up in her chair. "Skyler? What...are you doing here?"

Deacon glanced at her. "Skyler dropped by to have some breakfast with us."

Ruthie came in and set a plate in front of Skyler. "Sit down. Eat before it gets cold."

Skyler sat across from Abby and glanced at Tanner, who was grinning at him.

Deacon took his seat. "Tanner, do you have something to say?"

"No. I'm just eating my eggs." He busied himself with his plate.

Deacon looked at Skyler. "If you don't have anywhere to be, Tobias and I'd like to sit down with you and talk about what to do with Winston's place."

"I need to feed the horses. Then I can come right back."

"Abby. Are you free in a couple of hours? I'd like you in on the conversation, too."

"I'm totally free."

"Good. We'll all meet back here at one."

Skyler nodded and picked up his fork, then ventured a glance at Abby. She raised an eyebrow, before taking a sip of her coffee.

After breakfast, Skyler thanked Deacon, then nodded at Abby. She gave him a quick smile, and he stood to go. "I'll see you all at one o'clock."

He left the dining room and Deacon looked at Abby. "Are you going to make him walk all the way down the road to his car by himself?"

She smiled as she got to her feet. "We'll be back by one."

She left the house and ran to catch up to Skyler.

He took her hand and glanced back at the house. "Shit. Deacon caught me coming down the ladder."

"You're kidding. I just thought he saw you in the yard."

"Nope."

"So, he knows."

"Yeah. I'd say he knows."

"And once again, you're still alive. That's a good sign, right?"

He stopped walking and looked at her. "I'd consider it a good sign, yeah."

Abby put her arms around his neck and he put his hands on her waist. "I feel like a whole new universe has opened up for me. With you right in the center of it."

"Am I your sunshine?"

"You're my sun, my moon, all the stars. You're my world, Abby."

She kissed him and felt the fireworks go off around them. She pulled back and looked at him. "And now, my dear Skyler, you have to admit the fireworks are everything."

"The fireworks are definitely everything."

————————— ❧ —————————

They got back to the house by one and found Deacon in his office with Tobias and Tanner.

Abby smiled at Deacon. "Wow. The whole gang is here."

"This is a new chapter for the Starlight. It's only right that everyone is in on the decisions that need to be made."

He stood and went to the bar in the corner of the room. "We're going to drink bourbon because that was Dad's choice of alcohol. He gave me a shot on my twenty-first birthday in this room. We drank to the future of the Starlight." Deacon poured five shots and handed them out, then raised his glass. "To the future of the Starlight Ranch." They all drank their shots.

"We sign the papers for Winston's ranch in a couple weeks, which will add seventy-five-thousand acres to the Starlight. I've also been talking to Desmond Rafferty. He owns the sixty- thousand acres between the O'Hare ranch and the Starlight. Once I get that, and I will, we'll pretty much own half of the valley. And all the private land around Washburn Lake will be ours."

Skyler leaned forward in his seat. "Shit. That's damn impressive."

"We don't need Rafferty's place, but it'll connect the two ranches and give us some more grazing land. He hasn't lived there in years and the structures aren't worth repairing. But having control of the lake, at least the half that isn't on Forest Service land, is worth a lot."

Tobias grinned. "And Leo Fremont can languish in the number two spot of the Texas Ten until hell freezes over."

Skyler laughed. "I think from now on it's going to be the Texas Nine and the Carmichaels."

Tobias pointed at him. "You could be right."

Cassidy and Gemma came into the room. "Sorry, we're late. We had to wait for Ruthie to get back from town and watch the kids."

Deacon smiled. "It's okay. All you missed is the toast, which neither of you would've participated in anyway." The women sat down. "Now that we're all here, let's talk about Winston's ranch."

Skyler held up a finger. "As a bit of an outsider, can I say something?"

"The fact that I didn't shoot you this morning makes you an insider. Speak up."

Skyler glanced at Abby. "Tobias said you thought you might want to lean toward training."

"That's right."

"I think that's a great idea. You can do some buying and selling, but most of your income would come from the training. You're not investing anything but time and talent. And this family has plenty of that."

"What would we need to become a top training facility? One that clients will deem worthy of traveling to?"

"You'd have to expand the barn or build a second one. Put in some training pens. And build a professional sized arena, preferably an indoor one. That way we could train all year."

Cassidy nodded. "We could build it in the pasture next to the barn. It's flat and large enough to build whatever you want. There would be room for parking horse trailers. It'd be perfect."

Deacon nodded. "That would work." He looked at Tanner. "So, how do you feel about being a full-time trainer? Doing your horse whispering thing and getting these high-strung show horses to co-operate."

"Um...I'd love it. But aren't I going to be gone for a few years?"

Deacon glanced at Abby. "Don't get mad at me."

She raised an eyebrow. "About what?"

He turned to Tanner. "I figure you're a hell of a lot more valuable here than you would be at Yale getting a business degree." Tanner jumped to his feet, then went to Deacon and hugged him. Deacon laughed and patted his back. "What do you say?"

Tanner stepped away from him. "I say hell yeah."

Abby stood up and shook her head at Deacon, then hugged Tanner. Then she hugged Deacon, too. "Good for you. You finally get it."

"It only took me twelve years."

They spent the rest of the afternoon making plans and discussing logistics and possibilities. In the end, it was decided Abby, Skyler, and Tanner would be in charge of the horse operation. This would leave Tobias still in charge of the men and the cattle. With Deacon overseeing the business end of everything. He, Tobias, and Skyler would share the responsibility of the out-of-town meetings and horse auctions.

When they talked it all out, Deacon went to the bar again. "We started this meeting with a drink. Let's end it with one as well." He poured five shots and passed them out, then raised his glass. "To the Starlight Ranch horse training facility. With the three best horsemen I know, we can't lose."

They all drank their shots, then Skyler got to his feet. "I just want to thank you all for giving me a new home and a new family. I ah..."

Abby stood and hugged him. "We all love you, Skyler. Welcome to the family."

Tobias set his glass down. "I just have one question. Eighteen, twenty years from now when it's time for your first kid to go to college. Where are you going to send him?"

Abby laughed. "We're going to let him decides where or if he wants to go."

Deacon nodded. "Right. That sounds all noble right now. You just wait. The second you hold that kid in your arms, you'll start planning their education."

Abby shook her head. "Poor little Thea."

Chapter Twenty-Five

"You're not taking credit for my brilliant idea."

D eacon had spent the morning at his lawyer's office signing the final paperwork on the O'Hare ranch and the Rafferty place. It was official. They were in the horse training business. And they had the biggest ranch on the Texas panhandle. Leo Fremont had yet to find out. But Skyler knew the news wouldn't be well received. He was glad to be rid of his father and excited to be part of the Carmichael's new venture. He and Abby working together. What could be better than that?

Abby, Skyler, and Tanner sat on the edge of the rock cropping behind the waterfall, hanging their feet over the edge. Tanner leaned forward and looked at the water thirty feet below.

"Yeah, that's really far down there."

Abby nudged him. "It seems even farther on the way down."

"I have to do it, right? To save face."

Skyler shook his head. "No. You don't need to prove anything."

They'd come up there to celebrate their new partnership in the Carmichael horse training business. Skyler pulled a bottle of champagne out of the backpack he'd brought.

Tanner laughed. "Wow. Get me drunk first, then goad me into jumping."

"Maybe it won't hurt so much, then. But, seriously, man. We didn't come here to jump. We came here to drink to the three damned best horse trainers in the business. Or at least soon-to-be best damn trainers.

Tanner smiled. "I can't believe Deacon finally gave up on the whole stupid Yale thing."

Skyler looked at him. "You should go to Harvard."

Tanner grinned. "Man. If I had the least bit of interest in going anywhere, I totally would."

Abby put her arm through his. "You're not going anywhere. Skyler may be good with horse. But you can talk to them. We need you for the ornery ones."

Skyler was sitting on Tanner's other side. "She's right. We do. No school for you."

Tanner let out a whoop that echoed off the rock wall. "Hell, yeah. No school for me."

Skyler removed the foil from the cork, then the wire keeper. He wiggled the cork until he felt it begin to give way. "Okay, here it goes." He worked the cork off the rest of the way with a loud pop and a mist of champagne. Then he held up the bottle. "To the Starlight Ranch Equestrian Training Facility. Or whatever we decide to call it. He took a drink, then passed the bottle to Tanner. Tanner drank from it, then handed it to Abby.

She took a drink. "Yay, us!"

They sat for a few minutes sharing the bottle of champagne, then Tanner looked at the water below them again. "I'm going to do it."

Abby took his arm. "I don't want you to get hurt."

"Nobody else got hurt. Why would I?"

He started to get up, but Skyler put a hand on his shoulder. "Hold on."

"You going to try to stop me, too?"

"No. You can jump, but I have to ask you something first. Just in case."

"In case of what?"

"Of whatever. Just listen for a minute."

Tanner glanced at Abby, then turned toward Skyler. "Okay. I'm listening."

"I want to ask you if you'll be my best man."

Tanner cocked his head, then looked back at Abby. He turned to Skyler again. "Your what now?"

"My best man."

"You guys are getting married. Wait. You guys are getting married?"

He hugged Skyler, and Abby frowned.

"Hello. Bride here."

Tanner turned to her and hugged her too.

"Shit, guys. When did this happen?"

"The other night. But no one else knows. You're the first one we've told."

"Man. Finally. I'm always the last person to know anything. Now...this is a lot of pressure."

Abby laughed. "Are you sure you can handle it?"

He nodded. "Yeah. But why aren't you telling anyone?"

"We will. Probably at Sunday dinner when everyone's together."

"And when is this wedding going to happen?"

Abby shrugged. "We don't know yet."

"Well, you know it seems to be a Carmichael tradition to do it right away. Deacon and Cassidy got married eight months after they met. Tobias and Gemma, about a year, but he started asking her as soon as she moved to town."

"Well, Skyler and I have been officially together about six weeks, so we have time to carry out the tradition."

"Man, that's record timing on the engagement, though."

Skyler smiled. "Well, we figure we've known each other for almost two years, so we're counting that."

"Even though you were engaged to someone else for a couple of months during that time?"

"We don't count that."

"Okay. Whatever. Congratulations." He took a drink of champagne. "Okay. Now I'm going to jump." He handed the bottle to Abby, then got up and took off his boots.

Skyler looked at him. "Cell phone? Wallet?"

"I don't have either with me."

Abby and Skyler stood up, and Skyler nudged Tanner. "I'm going with you."

Abby folded her arms across her chest. "Skyler?"

"He's my best man. And my business partner. I'm not letting him go alone." He took off his boots and then took his phone out of his pocket and dropped it into one of them. "I'll let you go first, then I'll follow you."

Tanner nodded, then went to the edge of the ledge. He took a deep breath, then after glancing at Abby, he leapt off. He hollered all the way down and landed with a splash. He came up a moment later.

"Shit! I did it!" He looked up at Skyler. "Come on. The water's freezing." He started swimming for the shore, then stopped when he could stand. He hugged his body and shivered.

Skyler kissed Abby, then took a deep breath and jumped. He came up with a curse and looked up at Abby. "Are you going to join us, or what?"

Abby kicked off her boots, then went to the edge of the rock ledge. "Wait for me. I need you there when I land."

"I'm right here. I got you."

She held her breath, then jumped with a squeal. She landed a couple feet from Skyler, and he swam to her and grabbed her when she came up.

"Oh, my God. It's worse than the first time." Skyler helped her to shore, and they climbed out to Tanner, who was sitting on the edge of the water. They dropped down next to him.

Abby took a minute to catch her breath, then looked at the two men. "Okay. Let's make that the last time we do that."

They both nodded, and Tanner said, "Hell, yeah. Once was enough."

Abby wanted to take Skyler to the old, twisted oak where her parents' ashes were buried. They rode out on a warm morning at the end of June. When they arrived at the tree, they dismounted and tied the horses to a nearby tree, then went to the old oak.

Abby took Skyler's hand. "Mother, you know Skyler. You reintroduced us at the gala. Dad, you might remember him as that pesky Fremont kid. Well, he's not a kid anymore, and he's not too pesky. We're going to get married. And I can only hope we're as happy as the two of you were."

Skyler squeezed her hand, then brought it to his mouth and kissed the back of it. "Mr. and Mrs. Carmichael, I promise you I'll take care of your daughter. I love her. I'll treat her right. And I swear, I'll take out anyone who tries to do her harm."

Abby turned to him and put her arms around his neck. He pulled her in close. "Do you think they'll mind if I kiss you?"

"I don't think they'll mind at all." He kissed her, then took a step back. "I just got a brilliant idea."

"Brilliant, huh?"

"Yeah. This is where we should do it. Right here. This is where we should get married."

She looked at him for a moment, then glanced at the tree. "So, Mother and Dad can be at our wedding."

"Yeah. What do you think?"

"How would we get Pastor Joe out here?"

"He was a cowboy for years before he found God. He still rides."

"You're kidding. How did I not know that?"

"So, what do you say?"

"There's still the matter of getting Ruthie here. She doesn't ride."

Skyler thought for a moment. "She could double up with Cassidy or Gemma."

Abby patted him on the chest. "Oh my gosh. We should get married right here."

He laughed. "Oh no. You're not taking credit for my brilliant idea."

She hugged him. "It's perfect. I love it." She looked around. "We could all ride here, have the ceremony, then have a picnic lunch in the grass." She looked at him. "That'd be great, right? Is it too..."

"Perfect. It's perfect." He kissed her again.

She leaned back and looked at him. "There's just one thing we need to make the day complete."

"What's that?"

"Fireworks."

He smiled. "You know, a very wise woman once told me the fireworks are everything. She asked me why I'd want to spend my life with someone who didn't make me feel like I'm standing in the middle of a Fourth of July celebration?"

She smiled at him. "She sounds very smart. You should marry her."

"I plan on it. And what better time to do that than the Fourth of July?"

"Do you mean the Fourth of July that's just six days away?"

"Yeah. That's the one."

"Hmm. It is the Carmichael tradition to get married very quickly once you find your fireworks person."

"So, what do you say?"

"I say we should go back to the ranch and make sure no one makes plans for the Fourth of July."

"Let's go." They started for the horses, then Skyler stopped. "Wait. There's something I'd like to do if it's okay with you."

"What's that?"

He took his pocket knife out his pocket and went to the tree. "Do you think they'd mind sharing their tree with us?"

She shook her head. "I don't think they'd mind at all."

Skyler opened his blade and carved a heart into the tree, then put *S F + A C* in the middle of it. Underneath, he carved *Forever.*

Want to see what Tanner is up to? Tanner

https://www.amazon.com/dp/B0CBYB8CLD

More Books By Leigh Fenty

The Three Oaks Ranch Series

Memories Of You

The Good Son

The Wayward Son

Little Sis

The Carmichael Series

Deacon

Tobias

Abigale

Tanner

The Christmas Wedding

Faith's Journal

The Gracie Island Series

The Deputy

The Best Woman

The Chief

The Family Man

The Visitor

Love Notes

The Last Will And Testament Of Atticus Wainwright III

The Out of Focus Series

Out Of Focus

Out Of Luck

Out Of The Deep

Out Of Time

The John O'Leary Series

The Boy In The Yellow Wellies

The Man Without A Heart

Touch

A Change Of Plans

About the Author

Leigh spends her days with cute, sexy guys. Unfortunately, they're on paper. But still, not a bad way to spend your day. She also writes about strong, independent women, who can hold their own against these irresistible guys. She's not a pure romance writer, because she breaks the rules a bit. But that's the fun part. Leigh's stories have adventure, family relationships, and the struggles life throws at you sometimes. But boy always meets girl. They tussle a bit while they figure out what they really want. Then find their happily ever after. Even if it's not what they thought it was going to be.

Printed in Great Britain
by Amazon